BEE: THE PRINCESS OF THE DWARFS

BEE: THE PRINCESS OF THE DWARFS

ANATOLE FRANCE

Translated by Peter Wright

WILDSIDE PRESS

Published by Wildside Press LLC.
www.wildsidepress.com

CONTENTS

CHAPTER I

TELLS OF THE NEWS THAT A WHITE ROSE BRINGS TO THE COUNTESS OF THE WHITE MOOR

Setting on her golden hair a hood spread with pearls and tying round her waist the widow's girdle, the Countess of the White Moor entered the chapel where she prayed each day for the soul of her husband, killed by an Irish giant in single combat.

That day she saw, on the cushion of her praying-stool, a white rose. At the sight of it she turned pale and her eyes grew dim; she threw her head back and wrung her hands. For she knew that when a Countess of the White Moor must die she finds a white rose on her stool.

Knowing that the time had come for her to leave this world, where she had been within such a short space of time a wife, a mother, and a widow, she went to her room, where slept her son George, guarded by waiting women. He was three years old; his long eyelashes threw a pretty shade on his cheeks, and his mouth was like a flower. Seeing how small he was and how young, she began to cry.

"My little boy," she said in a faint voice, "my dear little boy, you will never have known me, and I shall never again see myself in your sweet eyes. Yet I nursed you myself, so as to be really your mother, and I have refused to marry the greatest knights for your sake."

She kissed a locket in which was a portrait of herself and a lock of her hair, and put it round her son's neck. Then a mother's tear fell on his cheek, and he began to move in his cradle and rub his eyes with his little fists. But the Countess turned her head away and fled from the room. Her own eyes were soon to close for ever; how could they bear to look into those two adorable eyes where the light of understanding had just begun to dawn?

She had a horse saddled and rode to the castle of the Clarides, followed by her squire, Freeheart.

The Duchess of the Clarides kissed the Countess of the White Moor:

"What good chance has brought you here, my dear?"

"It is an evil chance that has brought me; listen, dearest. We were married within a few years of each other, and we became widows by a similar misfortune. In these times of chivalry the best die soonest, and only monks live long. When you became a mother I had already been one for two years. Your daughter Bee is as beautiful as day, and nothing can be said against my son George. I like you and you like me. For I must tell you I have found a white rose on the cushion of my stool. I am going to die. I leave my son to you."

The Duchess was aware of the news that the white rose brings to the ladies of the House of White Moor. She began to cry, and promised in her tears to bring up Bee and George as sister and brother, and not to give anything to one without giving half to the other. Then the two ladies put their arms round each other, and went to the cradle where little Bee slept under light blue curtains, as blue as the sky. Without opening her eyes she moved her little arms, and as she opened her fingers five small pink beams appeared to come out of each sleeve.

"He will defend her," said the mother of George. "And she will love him," the mother of Bee answered. "She will love him," a small, clear voice repeated.

The Duchess recognised it as that of a spirit that had long lived under the hearthstone.

On her return to her manor the Lady of the White Moor divided her jewels among her maids, and, having anointed herself with odorous essences and put on her most beautiful clothes to honour that body which will rise again on the Day of Judgment, she laid herself down on the bed and went to sleep for ever.

CHAPTER II

HOW THE LOVES OF BEE OF THE CLARIDES AND GEORGE OF THE WHITE MOOR BEGAN

The ordinary lot of women is to be more good than beautiful or more beautiful than good. But the Duchess of Clarides was as good as she was beautiful, and she was so beautiful that the princes who had only seen her picture had wished to marry her. To all their proposals she answered:

"As I have but one soul I will never have but one husband."

Yet she only wore mourning for five years. Then she put off her long veil and her black clothes, for she did not like to depress those around her or to prevent them smiling or being merry in her presence. Her Duchy included large tracts of land, and lonely moors covered in all their vast extent with heather; also lakes where fishermen caught fish, some of which were magical, and mountains, terrible and lonely, beneath which the dwarfs lived in their underground kingdom.

In the government of the Clarides she followed the advice of an old monk who had escaped from Constantinople. His belief in the wisdom of men was small, for he had seen how brutal and perfidious they are. He lived shut up in a tower with his birds and his books, and there he performed his duties as counsellor, acting according to a very few principles. His rules were: "Not to revive old laws; to give way to the wishes of the people for fear of rebellion, but to give way as slowly as possible, because, when one reform is carried out, the public immediately demand another. Princes are deposed for giving way too quickly, just as they are for resisting too long."

The Duchess, understanding nothing at all about politics, let him do as he pleased. She was charitable, and, as she could not like all men, she was sorry for those unfortunate enough to be wicked. She helped the unhappy in every possible way, visited the sick, consoled widows, and provided for orphans.

She brought up her daughter Bee with the most charming wisdom. She taught this child only to take pleasure in doing good, consequently she could indulge her to any extent.

This amiable lady kept her promise made to the poor Countess of the White Moor. She acted as a mother to George and made no distinction between Bee and him. They grew up together and George found Bee to his taste, though rather small. One day, when they were still in their earliest childhood, he came to her and said:

"Will you play with me?"

"I would like to," said Bee.

"We will find some sand and make sand pies," said George.

So they made pies, but as Bee did not make hers very well, George hit her on the fingers with his spade. Bee uttered the most piercing shrieks, and the squire, Freeheart, who was walking in the gardens, said to his young Lord:

"It is not a deed worthy of a Count of the White Moor to beat young ladies, your Highness."

George's first impulse was to thrust his spade right through the body of the squire. But as the difficulties of this enterprise seemed insuperable, he fell back upon an easier course of action, which was to turn his face against a big tree and weep copiously.

In the meanwhile, Bee took good care to keep her tears flowing by digging her fists into her eyes; and, in her despair, she flattened her nose against the trunk of a neighbouring tree. When night began to cover the earth, George and Bee were still weeping, each in front of their tree. The Duchess of the Clarides had to take her daughter with one hand and George with the other to bring them back to the castle. Their eyes were red, their noses were red, their cheeks were shiny; their sobs and snuffles were heart-rending. They ate their supper with a good appetite; then each was put to bed. But as soon as the candle was blown out they slipped out of bed like little ghosts and kissed each other shouting with laughter. So the loves of Bee of the Clarides and George of the White Moor began.

CHAPTER III

WHICH DEALS WITH EDUCATION IN GENERAL, AND THAT OF GEORGE IN PARTICULAR

George grew up in this castle next to Bee, whom he called sister in the way of friendship, though he knew she was not so.

He had masters to teach him fencing, riding, swimming, gymnastics, dancing, hunting, falconry, tennis and generally all the arts. He even had a writing master, an old clerk, humble in his ways, but inwardly proud, who taught him various styles of handwriting. The more beautiful the style was, the more difficult it was to read. George found little pleasure, and consequently little benefit, either in the lessons of this old clerk or in those of an old monk who gave grammatical instruction, using the most barbarous terminology. George could not make out why he should take the trouble to learn a tongue he could talk by nature, which is called the mother tongue.

The only person he liked being with was the squire, Freeheart, who, having sought adventures all over the world, knew the customs of men and of beasts, described all sorts of countries, and composed songs he did not know how to write down. Freeheart was the only master who taught George anything, because he was the only one who liked him, and affectionate lessons are the only good lessons. But the two pedants, the writing master and the grammatical master, who hated each other with all their heart, united in a common hatred of the old squire, whom they accused of inebriety.

It was true that Freeheart was rather too fond of going to the tavern called the Tin-jug. There he forgot his cares and composed his songs. He was certainly in the wrong.

Homer composed songs even better than Freeheart, and Homer only drank spring water. As to troubles, everybody has them, and it is not drinking wine but giving happiness to others that effaces them.

But Freeheart was an old man grown grey in the wars, loyal and meritorious, and the two masters ought to have hidden his weakness instead of reporting them with exaggeration to the Duchess.

"Freeheart is a drunkard," said the writing master, "and when he comes back from the tavern called the Tin-jug, he describes in the road large S's as he walks. I may say that this is the only letter he has ever shaped, for this drunkard is an ignoramus, your Grace."

The grammatical master added:

"As he staggers along he sings songs that offend against every rule and follow no received form; he is totally ignorant of synecdoche, your Grace."

The Duchess had a natural dislike of meanness and tale-bearing. She did what all of us would have done in the same situation: she disregarded them at first, but as they kept on repeating their reports she ended by believing them and determined to remove Freeheart. However, to make his exile honourable she sent him to Rome to get the blessing of the Pope. What made this journey so long to the Squire Freeheart was the large number of taverns, haunted by musicians, which lay between the Duchy of the Clarides and the papal city. The story will show how soon the Duchess was to regret she had deprived the two children of their most reliable protector.

CHAPTER IV

TELLS HOW THE DUCHESS TOOK BEE AND GEORGE TO THE HERMITAGE AND OF THEIR MEETING AN HIDEOUS OLD WOMAN THERE

One morning, that of the first Sunday after Easter, the Duchess issued from the castle on her big chestnut horse, having on her left George of the White Moor, riding a jet-black pony who had a white star in the middle of his forehead, and, on her right, Bee, who had a pink bridle to govern a pony with a cream-coloured coat. They were going to hear Mass at the Hermitage. Soldiers carrying lances escorted them, and there was a press of people on the way to admire them. And really each of the three was very beautiful. The Duchess looked stately and sweet under her veil spangled with silver flowers and her loose cloak: the mild splendour of the pearls which embroidered her headdress was becoming to the face and to the soul of this beautiful person. Next to her George, with his waving hair and bright eye, looked quite handsome, and the soft, clear colour of Bee's face, who was riding on her other side, was a delicious pleasure to the eye; but nothing was more wonderful than the flow of her fair hair, bound in a ribbon embroidered with three golden lilies. It fell down her shoulders like the splendid mantle of youth and beauty. The good folk looked at her and each said to the other, "What a pretty young lady!"

The master tailor, old John, lifted his grandson Peter in his arms to show him Bee, and Peter asked whether she was alive, or whether she was not really a piece of waxwork. He could not understand that a creature so white and delicate could belong to the same species as he, little Peter, did, with his chubby, sunburnt cheeks and drab rustic smock laced at the back.

While the Duchess received these marks of respect with kindness, the two children showed the contentment of pride, George in his flush, Bee in her smile. This is why the Duchess said to them:

"These good people greet us very cheerfully. George, what do you think of it? And what do you, Bee?"

"That they do well," said Bee.

"And that it is their duty," said George.

"And for what reason is it their duty?" the Duchess asked. Seeing they gave no answer, she continued:

"I am going to tell you. From father to son, for more than three hundred years, the dukes of the Clarides, lance in rest, protected these poor people, who owe it to them that they can reap the harvest they have sown. For more than three hundred years every Duchess of the Clarides has spun wool for the poor, visited the sick, and held their babies over the baptismal font. That is why, children, you are greeted."

George thought: "The ploughman will have to be protected," and Bee: "I will have to spin wool for the poor."

So, conversing and reflecting, they made their way through meadows enamelled with flowers. A range of blue hills ran its indented line along the horizon. George stretched out his hand towards the East.

"Is not that a large shield of steel that I see over there?"

"It is rather a silver buckle as large as the moon," said Bee.

"It is neither a shield of steel nor a silver buckle, children," the Duchess answered, "but a lake shining in the sun. The face of the water, that from a distance looks as smooth as a mirror, is broken into innumerable waves. The banks of this lake that seem to you as clean as if they were cut out of metal are really covered with reeds, waving their light plumes, and with irises, whose flower is like a human eye among drawn swords. Each morning white mists cover the lake, which shines like armour under the midday sun. But you must not go near it, for the Sylphs live there who draw travellers down into their crystal manor."

And now they heard the tinkle of the Hermitage bell.

"Let us get off," said the Duchess, "and go on foot to the chapel. It was neither on their elephants nor their camels that the Wise Men of the East approached the Manger."

They heard the Hermit's Mass. An old woman, hideous and in rags, knelt next to the Duchess, who offered her holy water as they went out of church, and said:

"Take some, my good woman."

George was astonished.

"Do you not know," said the Duchess, "that you must honour the poor as the favourites of Jesus Christ? A beggar woman just like this one held you over the baptismal font with the good Duke of the Black Rocks, and similarly your little sister Bee had a beggar as a godfather."

The old woman, who had guessed the feelings of the little boy, leaned towards him, leering, and said:

"I wish you the conquest of as many kingdoms as I have lost, my prince. I have been Queen of the Island of Pearls and of the Mountains of Gold; every day I had fourteen different kinds of fish served at my table, and a little blackamoor to carry my train."

"And by what misfortune did you lose your islands and your mountains, my good woman?" asked the Duchess.

"I offended the dwarfs, who have carried me off from my States."

"Have the dwarfs so much power?" asked George.

"Living under the earth," the old woman said, "they know the virtue of stones, fashion metal, and discover springs."

The Duchess:

"And what did you do to vex them, good mother?"

The old woman:

"On a night of December one of them came to me to ask my permission to prepare a great New Year's supper in the kitchens of the castle, which were larger than a capitular hall, and furnished with stew and preserving and frying pans, pipkins, caldrons, boilers, ovens, gridirons, porringers, dripping-pans, meat screens, fish-kettles, pastry-moulds, jugs, goblets of gold and silver and of grained woods, not to speak of the turnspit skilfully wrought of iron, and the huge black kettle hanging to the pothook. He promised that nothing should be lost or damaged. I refused his request, and he withdrew muttering dark threats. Three nights after, which was that of Christmas, the same dwarf returned to the room in which I was sleeping; he was accompanied by a multitude of others, who pulled me from my bed, and carried me off in my nightshirt to an unknown land.

"This," they said to me on leaving, "this is the punishment of rich people who will not grant a portion of their treasures to the industrious and gentle nation of Dwarfs, who fashion gold and cause the springs to flow."

So spoke the toothless old woman, and the Duchess, having comforted her with words and money, again took the road to the Castle with her two children.

CHAPTER V

IS CONCERNED WITH WHAT YOU SEE
FROM THE KEEP OF THE CLARIDES

One day, not long after this, Bee and George, without being seen, climbed up the stairs of the Keep which rises in the middle of the castle. On reaching the platform they shouted loudly and clapped their hands. The view stretched over rolling downs, cultivated and cut up into small green and brown squares. On the horizon they could see hills and woods—blue in the distance.

"Little sister," cried George, "little sister, look at the whole earth."

"It is very big," said Bee.

"My professor," said George, "had taught me that it was big, but as Gertrude our governess says, seeing is believing."

They walked round the platform.

"Here is a marvellous thing, little brother," said Bee. "The castle is in the middle of the whole earth, and we, who are on the Keep, which is in the middle of the castle, are now in the middle of the whole world. Ha! ha! ha!"

And really the skyline was around the children like a circle of which the Keep was the centre.

"We are in the middle of the world. Ha! ha! ha!" George repeated.

Then both began to think.

"What a pity it is that the world is so big!" said Bee. "You can lose yourself in it and be separated from your friends."

George shrugged his shoulders.

"How nice it is that the world is so big! You can look for adventures in it. Bee, when I am grown up I mean to conquer those mountains which are right at the end of the earth. It is there that the moon rises. I will catch it as I go along and give it to you, my Bee."

"That's it," said Bee; "you will give it to me and I will set it in my hair."

Then they began to look for the places they knew as if on a map.

"I know perfectly where we are," said Bee (who knew nothing of the sort), "but I cannot guess what all those little square stones sown on the side of the hill are."

"Houses!" answered George; "those are houses! Don't you recognise, little sister, the capital of the Duchy of the Clarides? It is quite a big town; it has three streets, of which one is paved. We passed through it last week to go to the Hermitage. Don't you remember it?"

"And that winding stream?"

"That's the river. Look at the old stone bridge over there."

"The bridge under which we fished for lobsters?"

"The very one, which has in the recess the statue of the 'Headless Woman,' but you cannot see her from here because she is too small."

"I remember. Why has she no head?"

"Probably because she has lost it."

Without saying whether the explanation satisfied her, Bee kept her eyes fixed on the distance.

"Little brother, little brother, do you see what is shining near the blue mountains? It is the lake."

"It's the lake!"

They now remembered what the Duchess had told them of the lovely and dangerous waters, where the Sylphs had their manor.

"Let us go there," said Bee.

This decision overwhelmed George, who gaped and said:

"The Duchess has forbidden us to go out alone, and how can we get to this lake, which is at the end of the world?"

"How to get there I really don't know, but you ought to, who are a man and have a grammar master."

George was stung, and answered that it is possible to be a man, and even a fine man, without knowing all the roads in the world. Bee gave him a mincing, disdainful look, made him blush to the tips of his ears, and said to him primly:

"I am not the one who promised to conquer the blue mountains and to unhook the moon. I do not know the road to the lake, but I will find it; you see!"

"Ha! ha! ha!" said George, trying to laugh.

"You laugh like a booby, sir."

"Bee, boobies neither laugh nor cry."

"If they did they would laugh like you. I will go to the lake alone. And while I discover the lovely waters where the Sylphs live, you can stay at the castle all by yourself like a little girl. I will leave you my tapestry frame and my doll. Please take great care of them, George; please take great care of them."

George had pride. He felt the shame which Bee put upon him. With his head down, darkly, he cried in a muffled voice:

"All right! we will go to the lake!"

CHAPTER VI

TELLS HOW BEE AND GEORGE
WENT OFF TO THE LAKE

Next day, after lunch, when the Duchess had retired to her room, George took Bee by the hand.

"Come along," he said to her.

"Where?"

"Hush!"

They went down the stairs and crossed the courts. When they had passed the gate Bee asked a second time where they were going.

"To the lake," George answered decisively.

The mouth of the stupefied Miss Bee gaped. Was it sensible to go that distance, and in satin slippers? For her slippers were of satin.

"We must go there, and we need not be sensible."

Such was the lofty answer given by George to Bee. She had put him to shame, and now she pretended to be astonished. It was now his turn to refer her disdainfully to her doll. Girls goad a man into adventures, and then draw back. Her behaviour was disgraceful. She might stay behind, but he would go himself.

She took him by the arm. He pushed her away. She flung herself round the neck of her brother.

"Little brother!" she said sobbing, "I will follow you."

Her repentance was complete, and it moved him.

"Come along," he said, "but do not let us go by the town, we might be seen. We had better follow the ramparts and reach the high road by a short cut."

They went holding each other by the hand. George explained the scheme he had drawn up.

"We will follow the road we took to go to the Hermitage; we are certain to see it as we saw it last time, and then we will go straight to it across the field in a bee-line."

In a bee-line is a pretty country way of saying a straight line, but the name of the little maid occurring quaintly in the idiom made them laugh.

Bee picked flowers growing by the ditch: flowers of the mallow and the mullein, asters and oxeyes, making a posy of them; the flowers faded visibly in her little hands, and they looked pitiful when Bee crossed the stone bridge. As she did not know what to do with her posy, the idea occurred to her of throwing them in the water to refresh them, but she preferred to give them to the "Headless Woman."

She asked George to lift her in his arms to make her tall enough, and she placed her handful of country flowers in the folded hands of the old stone figure.

At a distance she turned her head and saw a dove on the shoulder of the statue.

They walked some time, and Bee said:

"I am thirsty."

"So am I," said George, "but the river is far behind us, and I can see neither stream nor spring."

"The sun is so hot, it must have drunk them all up; what shall we do?"

Thus they talked and complained, when they saw a country-woman with a basket full of fruit.

"Cherries," cried George. "What a pity it is that I have no money to buy any!"

"I have some money," said Bee.

She drew out of her pocket a purse with five pieces of gold in it, and addressed the country-woman.

"Good woman," she said, "will you give me as many cherries as my dress can carry."

As she spoke she held out the skirt of her frock with both hands. The countrywoman threw two or three handfuls of cherries into it. Bee took the fold of her skirt in one hand and with the other held out a piece of gold to the woman and said:

"Is that enough, that?"

The countrywoman seized the piece of gold, which would have been a high price for all the cherries in the basket, with the tree on which they had grown, and the orchard in which the tree was planted, and she cunningly answered:

"That will do to oblige you, my little Princess."

"Then," replied Bee, "put some more cherries in my brother's hat, and I will give you another gold piece."

This was done and the countrywoman pursued her way, thinking of the old stocking under the mattress in which she was to hide her two pieces of gold. And the two children went on their road eating the cherries, and throwing the stones to the right and the left. George looked for cherries held together in pairs by the stalk to make earrings of them for his sister, and he laughed to see the beautiful vermeil-coloured twin fruit swinging on the cheek of Bee.

A pebble checked their joyful progress. It had stuck in the slipper of Bee, who began to limp. At each hop she took her gold curls waved on her cheeks, and limping thus, she went and sat down. There her brother, kneeling at her feet, took off her satin slipper; he shook it, and a little white pebble rolled out.

Then looking at her feet, she said:

"Little brother, when we go again to the lake, we will put on boots."

The sun had by now declined in the radiant sky. A breath of wind fanned the necks and the cheeks of the young travellers who boldly, and with fresh alacrity, pursued their travels. To walk more easily, they held each other by the hand and sang, and they laughed to see their two black shadows, likewise united, moving in front of them. They sang:

Marian the maid,

Demure and staid,
Went riding to the mill,
She placed her load
Of corn, and rode
Upon her donkey Bill.
But Bee stops. She cries:
"I have lost my slipper, my satin slipper."

And it was as she said. The silk bows of the little slipper had got loose as she walked, and it lay all dusty in the road.

Then she looked behind her, and seeing the towers of the castle swimming in the distant mist, she felt a pang, and tears came into her eyes.

"The wolves will eat us," she said, "and our mother will never see us again, and she will die of grief."

But George brought her slipper to her and said:

"When the castle bell rings for supper, we will be back at the Clarides. Forward!"

The miller tight,
With flour white,
Stood close under the mill,
And fair and free.
Cried, "To that tree
Tie up your donkey Bill."

"The lake, Bee, look: the lake, the lake, the lake."

"Yes, George, the lake!"

George cried hurrah! and threw his hat in the air. Bee was too well behaved to throw up her coif in the same fashion. But taking off her slipper which barely held, she threw it over her head to show her joy. There it was, the lake, at the bottom of the valley the slopes of which ran round the silvery waters, holding them as in a cup of foliage and flowers. There it was, calm and clear, and a shiver still ran over the ruffled grasses of its banks. But the two children could not discover any road in the thickets to take them to this lovely mere. As they searched, their legs were bitten by geese, who were followed by a little girl, dressed in a sheepskin, with a switch in her hand. George asked her what she was called.

"Gill."

"Well, Gill, how do you go to the lake?"

"I don't go."

"Why?"

"Because."

"But if you did go?"

"If I did go, there would be a road, and I would take the road."

There was no answer to be given to the goose-girl.

"All right," said George, "we will certainly find a path in the wood further on."

"We will pick nuts there," said Bee, "and eat them, for I am hungry. We must, when we come again to the lake, bring a bag full of things good to eat."

George:

"We will do as you say, little sister. I now approve the plan of the squire Freeheart, who, when he set out for Rome, took with him a ham for hunger and a demijohn for thirst. But we must hurry, for it seems to me it is getting late, though I do not know the time."

"Shepherdesses know it by looking at the sun," said Bee; "but I am not a shepherdess. Yet it seems to me that this sun, which was above our heads when we started, is now over there, far behind the town and the land of the Clarides. I wish I knew whether this is the case every day, and what it means."

While they thus observed the sun a cloud of dust rose on the road, and they saw horsemen, who moved towards them at full gallop and whose armour glittered. The children were very frightened and went and hid in the underwoods. They are robbers, or rather ogres, they thought. But really they were men-at-arms sent by the Duchess of Clarides to search for the two little adventurers.

The two little adventurers found a narrow path in the under-wood which was not a lover's path, for two could not walk side by side holding each other by the hand, as lovers do. Further, the footprints were not human. Only a track made by a multi-tude of little hoofed feet was visible.

"These are the footprints of elves," said Bee.

"Or roedeer," said George.

The problem is as yet unsolved. But what is certain is that the path led by an easy descent to the edge of the lake, which now unfolded itself to the children in all its languid and silent beau-ty. Willows bent their tender foliage over it. Reeds, like pliant swords, swayed their delicate plumes on the water. They stood ruffling in islands, and around them the water-lilies spread their broad heart-shaped leaves and their pure white flowers. Over the flowering islands shrill dragon-flies flew, whirling and dart-ing, with emerald or sapphire breastplates and wings of flame.

And the two children enjoyed the exquisite pleasure of dip-ping their burning feet into the wet gravel where the thyme grew thick and the cattail darted its long spikes. From its lowly stem the iris yielded them its scent; all around the ribwort unrolled its lace on the edge of the sleeping waters which were studded with the loosestrife's purple flowers.

CHAPTER VII

SHOWS THE PENALTY GEORGE OF THE WHITE MOOR PAID FOR HAVING GONE NEAR TO THE LAKE WHERE LIVE THE SYLPHS

Bee went forward on the gravel between two clumps of willows, and in front of her the little genius of the place jumped into the water and made rings on its surface, which grew larger and larger till they vanished. This genius was a little green frog with a white stomach. All was silent: A fresh breath of wind swept over that clear lake, of which each wave rose in a gracious and smiling fold.

"This is a pretty lake," said Bee, "but my feet are bleeding in my little torn slippers, and I am very hungry. I wish I was in the castle."

"Little sister," said George, "sit on the grass. I am going to wrap your feet in leaves to cool them; then I will go and look for supper for you. I saw up there, close to the road, briars black with berries. I will bring you the largest and sweetest in my hat. Give me your handkerchief, I will fill it with strawberries, for there are plants close by the edge of the path, under the shade of the trees. And I will fill my pockets with nuts."

He made a bed of moss for Bee near the side of the lake, under a willow, and went off.

Bee lay with clasped hands on her bed of moss, and saw the stars kindle their tremulous lights in the pale sky; then her eyes half shut; yet she seemed to see in the air a little dwarf riding on a crow. This was not an illusion. The dwarf drew the bridle in the mouth of the black bird, stopped above the little girl, and fixed his round eyes on her. Then he struck his spurs, and went off at full flight. Bee saw these things confusedly and went to sleep.

She was sleeping when George came back with his harvest, which he put next to her. He then went down to the edge of the lake to wait till she woke. The lake was sleeping under its delicate crown of leafage. A light mist softly crept over it. All at once the moon showed itself between the branches and immediately the waters were strewn with points of light.

George plainly saw that the lights which glanced on the waters were not all broken reflections of the moon, for he noticed blue flames which came whirling nearer, and rose and fell and swayed as if they were dancing rounds. He soon discerned that these flames flickered on white foreheads, on the foreheads of women. In a short time lovely heads crowned with weed and shell, shoulders down which fell blue hair, bosoms glittering with pearls and from which veils were sliding, rose above the waves. The boy recognised the Sylphs, and tried to fly. But already pale, cold arms had seized him, and he was being carried, in spite of his struggles and screams, through the waters, in halls of crystal and porphyry.

CHAPTER VIII

SHOWS HOW BEE WAS TAKEN TO
THE LAND OF THE DWARFS

The moon had risen above the lake, and only the broken fragments of its orb were reflected in the water. Bee still slept. The dwarf who had examined her came back on his crow. This time he was followed by a troop of little men. They were very little men. They had white beards reaching down to their knees. They were the size of children, but they had old faces. The leather aprons and the hammers which they carried hanging at their belts made it evident they were metal-workers. They moved in a strange way by jumping to a great height and turning wonderful somersaults; this incredible nimbleness made them less like men than spirits. But in their wildest antics their faces remained unalterably grave, so that it was impossible to make out their real character.

They placed themselves in a circle round the sleeper.

"Well," said the smallest of the dwarfs from the height of his feathered mount; "well, I did not deceive you when I warned you that the prettiest of princesses was sleeping on the edge of the lake, and do you not thank me for having shown her to you?"

"We thank you, Bob," answered one of the dwarfs, who looked like an old poet; "truly, there is nothing in the world as pretty as this maiden. Her complexion is rosier than the dawn upon the mountains, and the gold of our smithies is not as bright as that of her tresses."

"It is true, Pic; Pic, nothing could be more true!" answered the dwarfs; "but what shall we do with this pretty maid?"

Pic, who resembled an old poet, did not answer this question of the dwarfs, because he did not know more than they did what to do with the pretty maid.

A dwarf, named Rug, said to them:

"Let us build a large cage and we will shut her in it."

Another dwarf, named Dig, opposed this suggestion of Rug. According to Dig, only wild beasts were put in cages, and as yet there was nothing to indicate that the pretty maiden was one of them.

But Rug was taken with his own idea, for want of another to put in its place. He ingeniously defended it:

"If this person," he said, "is not wild, she will doubtlessly become so by being shut in the cage, which will consequently become useful, and even indispensable."

This argument displeased the dwarfs, and one of them, named Tad, denounced it indignantly. He was a dwarf of utmost goodness. He proposed taking back the beautiful girl to her parents, whom he thought to be powerful lords.

This view of the good Tad was rejected as contrary to the custom of the dwarfs.

"Justice should prevail," Tad went on to say, "and not custom."

He was no longer listened to; the crowd had fallen into disorder and tumult, when a dwarf, called Paw, who was simple, but sensible, gave his views as follows:

"We must first wake the maiden, as she does not wake of herself. If she spends the night like this, to-morrow her eyelids will be swollen and her beauty will be less, for it is very unhealthy to sleep in a wood on the edge of a lake."

This opinion met with general approval, because it was not opposed to any other.

Pic, who resembled an old poet overwhelmed with misfortune, went near to the little maid and gazed on her gravely, with the idea that a single one of his looks would suffice to rouse the sleeper from the deepest sleep. But Pic over-estimated the power of his eyes, and Bee continued to sleep with her hands clasped.

Seeing this, the good Tad gently pulled her sleeve. Then she opened her eyes and raised herself on her elbow. Seeing herself on a moss-couch, surrounded by dwarfs, she thought that what she saw was a dream, and she rubbed her eyes to open them and to let in, instead of this fantastic vision, the bright early morning light streaming into her blue room, where she imagined herself to be. For her mind, numb with sleep, did not recall the adventure of the lake. But rub her eyes as she might, the dwarfs stayed there; she had to believe they were real. Then, looking round anxiously, she saw the forest, her memory returned, she cried in agony:

"George! my brother George!"

The dwarfs pressed round her, and, for fear of seeing them, she hid her face in her hands.

"George! George! where is my brother George?" she cried sobbing.

The dwarfs did not tell her, and for this reason, that they did not know. So she wept bitterly, calling on her mother and her brother.

Paw felt inclined to cry like her; but anxious to console her, he spoke a few vague words.

"Do not alarm yourself," he said. "It would be a pity if such a beautiful lady spoilt her eyes by crying. But rather tell us your history; it is certain to be interesting. It would give us the very greatest pleasure."

She was not listening. She rose and tried to run away. But her swollen, naked feet gave her such sharp pain that she fell on her knee and burst into still more violent sobs. Tad held her up in his arms, and Paw gently kissed her hand. This is why she dared to look and saw that their faces were compassionate. Pic seemed to be an inspired but innocent creature, and noticing that all the little men looked upon her with kindliness, she said to them:

"Little men, it is a pity you are so ugly; but I will like you all the same if you will give me something to eat, for I am hungry."

"Bob!" all the dwarfs cried at the same time, "fetch some supper."

And Bob went off on his crow. Still the dwarfs felt that this little girl had been guilty of an injustice in considering them ugly. Rug was extremely angry. Pic said to himself, "She is only a child, and does not see the fire of genius burning in my looks so as to give them alternately masterful strength and fascinating grace." Paw thought, "Perhaps it would have been better not to wake this young lady who considers us ugly." But Tad said, smiling:

"You will consider us less ugly, Miss, when you like us better."

At these words Bob reappeared on his crow. He brought a roast partridge on a gold dish, with a loaf of meal bread and a bottle of red wine. He placed this supper at the feet of Bee, turning an endless number of somersaults.

Bee ate and said:

"Little men, your supper is very good. My name is Bee; let us look for my brother, and go together to the Clarides, where Mama is waiting for us in a state of great anxiety."

But Dig, who was a good dwarf, urged on Bee that she was incapable of walking; that her brother was old enough to find himself; that no accident could happen to him in this country, where all wild beasts had been destroyed. He added:

"We will make a stretcher, we will cover it with a litter of leaves and mosses, we will place you on it, we will carry you thus into the mountain, to introduce you to the King of the dwarfs, as the custom of our people requires."

All the dwarfs applauded. Bee looked at her sore feet and was silent.

She was relieved to hear there were no wild beasts in the country. In all other matters she relied on the friendship of the dwarfs.

Already they were constructing the stretcher. Those who had axes were hacking away at the stems of two young pines.

This revived his idea in the head of Rug.

"If, instead of a stretcher," he said, "we built a cage?"

But he raised a unanimous protest. Tad, looking at him with contempt, exclaimed:

"Rug, you are more like a man than a dwarf. But this, at least, is to the credit of our race that the wickedest of the dwarfs is also the stupidest."

Meanwhile, the work went on. The dwarfs leapt in the air to reach branches which they cut in their flight, and out of which they neatly built a lattice chair. Having covered it with moss and dry leaves, they made Bee sit there; then, all together, they seized the two poles, up! hoisted it on their shoulders, and swung off to the mountain.

CHAPTER IX

TELLS FAITHFULLY THE WELCOME GIVEN BY KING LOC TO BEE OF THE CLARIDES

They ascended the woody side of the hill by a tortuous path. Here and there blocks of granite, bare and rusty, rose in the grey foliage of the dwarf oaks, and the rugged landscape was enclosed by russet hills and their blue-grey ravines.

The procession, preceded by Bob on his winged steed, entered a cleft of the rocks hung with briar. Bee, with her golden hair scattered on her shoulders, looked like the dawn risen on the mountains, if it is true that sometimes the dawn gets frightened, calls for her mother, and tries to run away, for these three events occurred when the little girl dimly saw dwarfs terribly armed lurking in all crevices of the cliff.

They held themselves motionless with their bows strung and levelled lances. Their tunics of hide and long knives hanging at their belts gave them a terrible appearance. Game of fur and feather lay at their feet. But these hunters, as far as their faces went, did not look fierce; on the contrary, they seemed mild and grave like the dwarfs of the forest, whom they very much resembled.

Upright in their midst stood a dwarf of great majesty. He wore a cock's feather at his ear, and on his forehead a diadem studded with enormous jewels. His mantle was flung over his shoulder showing a robust arm, loaded with gold rings. A bugle of ivory and carved silver hung at his belt. He leant his left hand upon his lance in an attitude of repose and strength, and with the right he shielded his eye to look towards Bee and the light.

"King Loc," the dwarfs of the forest said to him, "we bring you the beautiful little girl we have found: her name is Bee."

"You do right," said King Loc. "She will live among us, as the custom of the dwarfs requires."

Then advancing to Bee,

"Bee," he said to her, "welcome!"

He spoke gently to her, for already his feelings towards her were friendly. He stood on tiptoe to kiss her hand which hung down, and re-assured her that not only should no kind of harm happen to her, but that all her wishes should be satisfied, even if she should ask for necklaces, mirrors, wool of Cashmere, and silks of China.

"I would very much like some slippers," answered Bee.

Then King Loc struck a gong of bronze which hung to the walls of rock with his lance, and immediately something was seen coming from the end of the cavern bounding like a ball. It grew bigger till it became a dwarf, the features of whose face recalled those given by painters to the illustrious Belisarius, but whose leather apron showed him to be a bootmaker.

As a matter of fact it was the chief bootmaker.

"True," said the King to him, "choose in our store the most supple leather, take cloth of gold and silver, ask the keeper of my treasures for a thousand pearls of the finest water, and construct a pair of slippers for little Bee out of the leather, the tissues and the pearls."

At these words True threw himself at the feet of Bee and measured them accurately. But she said:

"Little King Loc, you must give me the beautiful slippers you have promised me directly, and, when I have them, I will return to my mother at the Clarides."

"You will have your slippers, Bee," answered King Loc: "you will have them to walk about inside the mountain and not to return to the Clarides, for you cannot leave this kingdom where you will learn beautiful secrets that are unguessed upon the earth. Dwarfs are superior to men, and it is for your happiness that you have been found by them."

"It is for my unhappiness," answered Bee. "Little King Loc, give me wooden shoes like those worn by peasants, and let me return to the Clarides."

But King Loc shook his head to express that it was not possible. Then Bee clasped her hands and sweetened her voice:

"Little King Loc, let me go and I will love you."

"You will forget me, Bee, on the sunny earth."

"Little King Loc, I will not forget you, and I will love you as much as Breath-of-Wind."

"And who is Breath-of-Wind?"

"My cream-coloured pony; he has a pink bridle and eats out of my hand. When he was small, the squire Freeheart used to bring him up to my room of a morning, and I used to kiss him. But now Freeheart is at Rome and Breath-of-Wind is too big to go upstairs."

King Loc smiled.

"Bee, will you love me more than Breath-of-Wind?"

"I will."

"That is right."

"I will, but I cannot; I hate you, little King Loc, because you prevent me seeing my mother and George again."

"Who is George?"

"George is George, and I like him."

The friendship of King Loc for Bee had largely increased in a few moments, and, as he already hoped to marry her when she was of age, and through her to reconcile men and dwarfs, he feared that George might at some time become his rival and disturb his plans. This is why he knit his eyebrows and walked off, drooping his head like a worried man.

Bee, seeing she had vexed him, gently plucked at the skirt of his coat.

"Little King Loc," she said in a sad and tender voice, "why do we each of us make the other unhappy?"

"Bee, it is the fault of circumstances," answered King Loc; "I cannot take you back to your mother, but I will send her a dream which will inform her of your fate, dear Bee, and console her."

"Little King Loc," answered Bee, smiling through her tears, "you have had a good idea, but I will tell you what you ought to do. Every night you ought to send my mother a dream in which she will see me and send me a dream in which I will see my mother."

King Loc promised to do so. And what he said he did. Each night Bee saw her mother, and each night the Duchess saw her daughter. This satisfied their affection a little.

CHAPTER X

IN WHICH THE WONDERS OF THE KINGDOM OF THE DWARFS ARE THOROUGHLY DESCRIBED, AS WELL AS THE DOLLS WHICH WERE GIVEN TO BEE

The kingdom of the dwarfs was deep and stretched under a great part of the earth. Though the sky was only visible here and there through openings in the rock, the open places, the roads, the palaces, and hall were not buried in the thickest night. Only a few rooms and several caverns remained in darkness. The others were lighted, not by lamps and torches, but by planets and meteors which shed a wild, fantastic brightness, and this brightness shone upon strange marvels. Enormous buildings had been hewn in the face of the rock: in certain places palaces cut out of granite rose to such a height up under the vaults of the huge caverns that their stone carvings disappeared in a mist pierced by the yellowish light of little planets less luminous than the moon.

There were in those kingdoms fortresses of stupendous mass, amphitheatres whose stone tiers formed a semicircle which the eye could not embrace in its full extent, and vast wells with sculptured sides in which no plummet could ever have found a bottom. All these structures, apparently unsuited to the stature of their inhabitants, agreed perfectly with their quaint fantastic turn of mind.

The dwarfs wrapped in hoods with sprigs of fern-leaves stuck in them moved about these buildings with the nimbleness of spirits. It was quite common to see one jump from the height of two or three stories on to the lava pavement and rebound like a ball. His face retained in the act that calm, majestic expression which sculptors give to the heads of ancient great men.

There was no indolence, and all applied themselves to their work. Whole quarters resounded with the noise of hammers; the shrieks of machinery echoed against the cavern roofs, and it was a curious sight to see the crowd of miners, smiths, goldbeaters, jewellers, diamond polishers, handle their pickaxes, hammers, pincers, and files with the dexterity of monkeys. But there was a more peaceful quarter.

There, uncouth and huge figures, shapeless pillars dimly projected from the rough stone; they seemed to be aged and venerable. There rose a squat palace with low doors; it was the palace of King Loc. Just opposite was the house of Bee, house, or rather cottage, with only one room in it, and this was hung with white muslin; fir-wood furniture spread its pleasant scent in the room. A cleft in the rock let in the light of the sky, and on fine nights stars were visible.

Bee had no special servants, but the whole dwarf nation struggled in emulation to supply all her needs and anticipate all her wishes, except that of reascending above ground.

The most learned dwarfs who possess great secrets took pleasure in teaching her, not with books, for dwarfs do not write, but by showing her all the plants of the mountains and the valleys, the different kinds of animals, and the various stones which are drawn from the bosom of the earth. And it was by sights and examples that they, with their gay simplicity, taught her the wonders of nature and the methods of art.

They made toys for her such as no rich children on the earth have ever had, for these dwarfs were capable and invented marvellous machines. In those depths they put together for her dolls that could move with grace and express themselves according to the rule of poetry. When assembled in a little theatre, of which the scenery represented the sea shore, the blue sky, palaces, and temples, these dolls played tragedies of surpassing interest. Though they were not much longer than a man's arm they looked exactly, some like reverend old men, others like men in the prime of life, or like lovely maidens dressed in white robes. There were also among them mothers clasping to their bosoms innocent little children. And these eloquent dolls spoke and acted on the stage as if they were moved by hatred, love, or ambition. They passed cleverly from joy to grief, and so well did they imitate nature that they raised smiles or drew tears. Bee clapped her hands at the show. The dolls who aimed at tyranny made her shudder with disgust. On the other hand she poured treasures of compassion on the doll who, once a princess, now a widow and a captive, her head crowned with cypress, has no other means of saving the life of her child than marrying, alas! the barbarian who made her a widow.

Bee never grew tired of this game in which the dolls introduced infinite variety. The dwarfs also gave concerts for her and taught her to play the lute, the viola, the theorbo, the lyre, and divers other kinds of instruments. In such a fashion she became a good musician, and the plays represented by the dolls gave her an experience of men and life. King Loc was present at these plays and concerts, but he saw and heard no one else but Bee, and his whole soul was gradually drawn towards her.

Meanwhile days and months passed, years made their round, and still Bee stayed among the dwarfs, incessantly amused and always full of regret for the earth. She was growing into a beautiful young woman. Her strange fate gave a touch of strangeness to her face, only adding to it another charm.

CHAPTER XI

IN WHICH THE TREASURE OF KING LOC IS DESCRIBED AS WELL AS POSSIBLE

Bee had been among the dwarfs for six years to a day. King Loc summoned her to his palace and ordered his treasurer in her presence to displace a large stone which seemed fixed in the wall, but which was, in reality, only inserted into it.

They all three passed through the opening left by the removal of the large stone and found themselves in a crevice of the rock where two people could not walk abreast. King Loc went forward first along the dark path and Bee followed, holding on to the skirt of the royal mantle. They went on walking for a long time. At times the walls of rock came so close together that the girl was afraid of being caught between them, without being able to move forward or back, and of dying there. But the mantle of King Loc sped before her along the dark and narrow path. At last King Loc found a bronze door, which he opened, and there was a flood of light.

"Little King Loc," cried Bee, "I never knew before that light was such a beautiful thing."

But King Loc, taking her by the hand, led her into the hall from which the light came, and said to her:

"Look!"

Bee, dazzled, at first saw nothing, for this huge hall, resting on high marble pillars, was from the floor to the roof all glorious with gold.

At the far end, on a dais made of sparkling gems, enchased in gold and in silver, and the steps of which were covered by a carpet of marvellous embroidery, was set a throne of ivory and gold with a canopy of translucent enamels. At its side two palm-trees, three thousand years old, rose from two gigantic vessels carved long ago by the best craftsmen of the dwarfs. King Loc sat down on this throne and made the young girl stand on his right hand.

"Bee," he said to her, "this is my treasure; choose whatever you like."

Immense shields of gold, hung to the pillars, caught the sunbeams and flung them back in dazzling showers. Crossed swords and lances hung flaming their bright points. The tables which spread close to the walls were loaded with bowls, flagons, ewers, chalices, pyxes, patins, goblets, beakers, with drinking-horns of ivory ringed with silver, with enormous bottles of rock crystals, dishes of carved gold and silver, with coffers, with reli-quaries in the shape of churches, with mirrors, with candelabra and censers as wonderful for their workmanship as for their ma-terial, and with thuribles in the shape of monsters, and on one of the tables a game of chess made of moonstones was spread out.

"Choose, Bee," King Loc repeated.

But raising her eyes above these riches, Bee saw the blue sky through an opening in the roof, and as if she had understood that the light of the sky alone gave these things their brightness, she only said:

"Little King Loc, I would like to go back to earth."

Then King Loc made a sign to his treasurer, who, lifting some heavy curtains, showed a huge coffer barred with plates and patterns of iron. The coffer being open there streamed from it a thousand beams of various and charming colours; each of these beams sprang from a precious stone cunningly cut. King Loc dipped his hand in them, and they saw rolling in luminous confusion the violet amethyst and the maiden stone; the em-erald of three natures, the one dark green, the other called the honeyed emerald because it is of the colour of honey, the third of a bluish-green called beryl, which bestows beautiful dreams; the eastern topaz; the ruby beautiful as the blood of brave men;

the dark blue sapphire called the male sapphire, and the pale blue sapphire called the female sapphire; the alexandrite, the hyacinth, the turquoise, the opal, whose lights are softer than those of the dawn, the hyalite, and the Syrian garnet. All the stones were of the most limpid water and the most luminous colour. And big diamonds cast their dazzling white lights among these coloured fires.

"Bee, choose," said King Loc.

But Bee shook her head and said:

"Little King Loc, I prefer a single one of the sunbeams which strike the slates of the castle of the Clarides to all these jewels."

Then King Loc had a second coffer opened which held nothing but pearls. But all these pearls were round and pure; their changing lights took on all the tints of the sky and the sea, and their glow was so mild that it seemed to express a lovely thought.

"Take some," said King Loc.

But Bee answered him:

"Little King Loc, these pearls remind me of the looks of George of the White Moor; I like these pearls but I like the eyes of George better."

Hearing these words, King Loc turned away his head. Yet he opened a third coffer and showed the young girl a crystal in which a drop of water had been a prisoner since the earliest time of the world, and, when shaken, the crystal showed this drop of water moving. He also displayed to her pieces of yellow amber in which insects more dazzling than jewels had been taken for millions of years. Their delicate legs and frail membranes were distinguishable, and they would have taken wing again if some power had melted like ice their scented prison-house.

"These are great natural curiosities; I give them to you, Bee."

But Bee answered:

"Little King Loc, keep the amber and the crystal, for I could not give back their liberty either to the fly or the drop of water."

King Loc looked at her for a time and said:

"Bee, the richest treasures will be well placed in your hands. You will possess them and they will not possess you. The greedy are the prey of their own gold; only those who despise wealth can possess it with safety; their souls will always be greater than their fortune."

Having thus spoken, he made a sign to his treasurer who presented a crown of gold on a cushion to the young girl.

"Receive this jewel as a sign of the esteem we have for you, Bee," said King Loc. "Henceforward you will be called the Princess of the Dwarfs."

And he himself placed the crown on the brow of Bee.

CHAPTER XII

IN WHICH KING LOC PROPOSES

The dwarfs celebrated the coronation of their first princess by festivals and rejoicings. In their perfect simplicity they played games at random in the huge amphitheatre, and the little men, with a sprig of fern or two oak leaves neatly fixed in their hood, went leaping joyfully along the subterranean streets. The rejoicings lasted thirty days. In his intoxication Pic had the look of an inspired mortal; the good Tad was enraptured with the general happiness; the tender Dig gave himself the pleasure of shedding tears; Rug, in his joy, again proposed that Bee should be put in a cage that the dwarfs might not fear losing so delightful a princess; Bob, riding on his crow, filled the air with such joyful cries that the bird itself grew merry, and gave forth wild little croaks.

King Loc alone was sad.

It came to pass that on the thirtieth day, having entertained the princess and the whole nation of the dwarfs at a splendid feast, he stood upon his arm-chair, and his kind face being thus raised to the level of Bee's ear:

"Princess Bee," he said to her, "I am going to make a request which you have full liberty to grant or to refuse. Bee of the Clarides, princess of the dwarfs, will you be my wife?"

And, speaking thus, King Loc, grave and tender, looked as handsome and mild as a majestic poodle. Bee pulled his beard and answered him.

"Little King Loc, I am willing to be your wife for fun; but I will never be your wife seriously. When you propose to marry me, you make me think of Freeheart, who, on the earth, used to tell me the most incredible tales to amuse me."

At these words King Loc turned away his head, but too slowly for Bee not to see a tear caught in the eyelashes of the dwarf. Then Bee was sorry she had hurt him.

"Little King Loc," she said to him, "I love you like a little King Loc that you are, and if you make me laugh as Freeheart used to, that ought not to annoy you, for Freeheart sang very well, and would have been good-looking without his grey hair and red nose."

King Loc answered her:

"Bee of the Clarides, princess of the dwarfs, I love you in the hope that you will one day love me. But had I not that hope I would love you just as much. I request you, in return for my friendship, always to be sincere with me."

"Little King Loc, I promise you I will."

"Well, Bee, tell me if you love any one enough to marry him."

"Little King Loc, I love no one as much as that."

Then King Loc smiled, and seizing his golden goblet he proposed in ringing tones the health of the princess of the dwarfs. And a vast murmur rose from the depths of the earth, for the table at which they feasted stretched from one end to the other of the dwarfish empire.

CHAPTER XIII

TELLS HOW BEE SAW HER MOTHER
AND COULD NOT KISS HER

Bee, with a crown set on her forehead, was more pensive and more sad than in those days when her hair flowed unbound on her shoulders, and when she went laughing to the smithy of the dwarfs to pull the beards of her good friends, Pic, Tad, and Dig, whose faces, reddened by the glow of the flames, grew merry at her welcome. The good dwarfs, who once used to dandle her on their knees and call her their Bee, now bowed at her approach and kept deferentially silent. She regretted she was no longer a child, and she was oppressed by being the princess of the dwarfs.

It no longer gave her any pleasure to see King Loc since she had seen him cry on her account. But she liked him; for he was kind, and he was unhappy.

One day (if it can be said that there are days in the empire of the dwarfs) she took King Loc by the hand and drew him to the fissure of the rock admitting a beam in which golden motes danced gaily.

"Little King Loc," she said to him, "I am in pain. You are also a king, you love me, and I am in pain."

Hearing these words of the beautiful maiden, King Loc answered:

"I love you, Bee of the Clarides, princess of the dwarfs; and this is why I have kept you in this our world, so as to teach you our secrets which are more great and wonderful than anything you can learn on earth among men, for men are less clever and less learned than dwarfs."

"Yes," said Bee, "but they are more like me than the dwarfs; that is why I like them better. Little King Loc, let me see my mother again, if you do not wish me to die."

King Loc walked away without answering.

Bee, alone and dejected, gazed on the beam of that light which bathes the whole face of the earth and pours its radiant floods on all living men, and even on the beggars that tramp the roads. Slowly the beam grew faint and changed its golden splendour into a pale, blue light. Night had come upon earth. A star glittered through the fissure in the rock.

Then some one touched her on the shoulder and she saw King Loc wrapped in a black mantle. On his arm hung another mantle which he put round the girl.

"Come," he said to her.

And he led her from underground. When she again saw the trees swept by the wind, the clouds racing over the moon and the whole of the fresh, blue night, when she smelt the scent of the grasses, and took to her bosom in a flood the air she had breathed during her childhood, she gave a great sigh and thought to die of joy.

King Loc had taken her in his arms; small as he was, he carried her as easily as a feather, and the two went gliding over the earth like the shadow of two birds.

"Bee, you are going to see your mother again. But listen. Every night, as you know, I send your image to your mother. Every night, she sees your dear shape. She smiles and speaks to it, and kisses it. To-night I am going to show you, instead of your ghost. You will see her; but do not touch her, do not speak of her, for then the charm would be broken, and she will never again see you nor your image, which she does not distinguish from yourself."

"I will therefore be careful, alas! little King Loc...there it is, there it is!"

There was the Keep of the Clarides rising black on the hill. Bee hardly had time to send a kiss to the old, well-beloved stones; now she saw, blooming with gilliflowers, the ramparts of the town of the Clarides fly past her; now she was going up along a slope where glow-worms shone in the grass to the postern gate, which King Loc opened easily, for the dwarfs, the metal workers, are not stopped by locks, padlocks, bolts, chains, and bars.

She went up the spiral staircase leading to her mother's room and stopped to put her two hands to her beating heart. The door opened slowly, and, by the light of a lamp hung from the ceiling, Bee saw, in the brooding, religious silence, her mother, worn and pale, her hair silvered at the temples, but more beautiful thus for her daughter than in the days gone by of splendid jewels and fearless rides. As the mother saw her daughter in a dream, she opened her arms to embrace her. And the child, laughing and sobbing, tried to cast herself into these open arms; but King Loc tore her from this embrace and carried her off like a straw over the dark champaign, down into the kingdom of the dwarfs.

CHAPTER XIV

IN WHICH THE GREAT GRIEF THAT
OVERTOOK KING LOC IS SEEN

Bee, seated on the granite steps of the subterranean palace, again gazed at the blue sky through the fissure in the stone. High above the elder trees turned their white umbels towards the light. Bee began to cry. King Loc took her by the hand and said to her:

"Bee, why are you crying and what do you want?"

And, as she had been sad for several days, the dwarfs seated at her feet were playing to her very simple tunes on the flute, the flageolet, the rebec, and the cymbals. Other dwarfs turned, to please her, such somersaults, that one after the other they stuck in the ground the tips of their hoods decorated with a plume of leaves; nothing could be more diverting to see than the sports of these little men with their hermit beards. The good Tad, the romantic Dig, who loved her from the day they had seen her sleeping on the edge of the lake, and Pic, the old poet, took her gently by the arm and begged her to tell them the secret of her grief. Paw, who was simple but sensible, held up to her grapes in a basket, and all, tugging the edge of her dress, repeated with King Loc:

"Bee, princess of the dwarfs, why are you weeping?"

Bee answered:

"Little King Loc and you all, little men, my grief increases your grief because you are kind; you weep when I weep. Know that I weep thinking of George of the White Moor, who must to-day be a brave knight, and whom I shall never see again. I love him and I wish to be his wife."

King Loc drew his hand from the hand he was pressing and said:

"Bee, why did you deceive me and tell me, at the feast table, that you loved no one?"

Bee answered:

"Little King Loc, I did not deceive you at the feast table. I did not then wish to marry George of the White Moor, and it is to-day my highest desire that he should propose to marry me. But he will not propose, since I do not know where he is and he does not know where to find me. And this is why I cry."

At these words the musicians stopped playing their instruments; the leapers interrupted their leaps and remained motionless on their heads or their seats; Tad and Dig shed silent tears on Bee's sleeve; the simple Paw let drop the basket with the bunches of grapes, and all the little men gave fearful groans.

But the King of the Dwarfs, more dejected than all of them under his crown of sparkling stones, walked away without a word, letting his mantle drag behind him like a torrent of purple.

CHAPTER XV

RELATES THE WORDS OF THE LEARNED NUR WHICH GAVE AN EXTRAORDINARY PLEASURE TO LITTLE KING LOC

King Loc had not shown his weakness to the maiden, but when he was alone, he sat on the ground, and holding his feet in his hands, he gave way to grief.

He was jealous, and he said to himself:

"She is in love, and it is not with me! Yet I am a king and am full of learning; I have treasures, I know marvellous secrets; I am better than all the other dwarfs, who are superior to men. She does not love me, and she loves a young man who has not the learning of the dwarfs and who, perhaps, has none at all. Clearly she does not appreciate merit and is silly. I ought to laugh at her want of sense, but I love her and nothing in the world pleases me because she does not love me."

For many long days King Loc wandered alone in the wildest gorges of the mountains, revolving in his mind sad and sometimes wicked ideas. He thought of compelling Bee by captivity and hunger to become his wife. But discarding the idea almost as soon as he had formed it, he determined to go to the girl and to throw himself at her feet. Still he could not make up his mind, and did not know what to do. For truly, the power was not given to him to make Bee love him.

His anger turned all at once against George of the White Moor; he hoped that this young man would be carried far away by a magician, or at least, if he should ever be acquainted with Bee's love, that he would disdain it.

And the king thought:

"Without being old, I have already lived too long not to have suffered at times. But my suffering, deep as it was, was never so fierce as what I undergo to-day. These former pains being caused by tenderness or by pity had something of their heavenly gentleness. On the contrary, I feel at this hour that my grief has the blackness and bitterness of a bad passion. My soul is arid, and my eyes swim in tears as in a burning acid."

So thought King Loc. And, dreading that jealousy should make him unjust and wicked, he avoided meeting the young girl for fear of using, without wishing to, the tone of a weak or violent man.

One day, being more than ordinarily tortured by the thought that Bee loved George, he determined to consult Nur, who was the most learned of the dwarfs and lived in the bottom of a well dug in the entrails of the earth.

This well had the advantage of an even, mild temperature. It was not dark, for two little planets, a pale sun and red moon, alternately gave light to every part of it. King Loc went down this well and found Nur in his laboratory. Nur had the face of a pleasant old little man, and carried a wisp of wild thyme in his hood. In spite of his learning, he showed in all matters the innocence and candour of his race.

"Nur," said the king, embracing him, "I have come to consult you because you know many things."

"King Loc," answered Nur, "I might know many things and yet be only a fool. But I know the way to learn a few of the innumerable things I do not know, and this is why I am justly renowned as a man of learning."

"Well," continued Loc, "do you know where a boy called George of the White Moor is now?"

"I do not know, and I have never had the curiosity to learn," answered Nur. "Knowing how ignorant, stupid, and wicked men are, I do not care much what they think or what they do. Except that, to give some value to the life of the proud and wretched race, the men have courage, the women beauty, and the little children innocence, O King Loc, the whole of mankind is lamentable or ridiculous. Subject like the dwarfs to the necessity of working to live, men have rebelled against the divine law, and, far from being like us workmen full of jubilance, they prefer war to work, and would rather kill than help each other. But one must acknowledge, to be just, that the brevity of their life is the principal cause of their ignorance and their ferocity. They live too short a time for them to learn how to live. The Dwarf race, which lives under the earth, is happier and better. If we are not immortal, at least each of us will last as long as the earth which carries us in its bosom and pervades us with its inmost, fruitful warmth, while for the race which is born on its rough rind, its breath is burning or icy, spreading death as well as life. However, men are indebted to their extreme misery and wretchedness for a quality which makes the soul of some of them more beautiful than the soul of the dwarfs. This quality, as splendid to the mind as the mild sheen of pearls to the eye, King Loc, is compassion. Suffering teaches it, and the dwarfs do not know it well, because, being wiser than men, they have fewer sorrows. So the dwarfs sometimes leave their deep grottoes and mix with men on the inclement rind of the earth, in order to love them, to suffer with them and through them, and then to taste compassion, which falls on the soul like a heavenly, refreshing dew. Such is the truth about men, King Loc; but did you not ask me for the particular fate of one of them?"

King Loc having repeated his question, the old Nur looked into one of the glasses that filled the room. For the dwarfs have no books, those found among them come from man and are used as toys. To instruct themselves they do not refer as we do to signs made upon paper; they look into the glasses and see the subject of their researches. The only difficulty is to select the proper glass and direct it rightly.

These glasses are of crystal, also of topaz and opal; but those which have a big polished diamond as lens are the most powerful and are used to see very distant things.

The dwarfs also have lenses of a diaphanous substance, unknown to men. These allow the eye to pierce through walls and rocks as if they were glass. Others, more wonderful still, reproduce as faithfully as a mirror all that time has carried away in its course, for the dwarfs can recall, from the infinite vastness of the ether back into their cavern the light of former days together with the shapes and colours of vanished ages. They enjoy this view of the past by collecting the showers of light, which, having once fallen against the forms of men, of beasts, of plants and of rocks, recoil through the immeasurable ether for all time.

The old Nur excelled in reviving the shapes of the past and even those, impossible to imagine, which existed before the earth had taken upon it the aspect which we know. So it was mere play for him to find George of the White Moor.

Having looked for less than a minute in quite a simple glass, he said to King Loc:

"King Loc, he whom you seek is now among the Sylphs, in the manor of crystal from which none return, and whose iridescent walls march with your kingdom."

"He is there, is he? Let him stop there!" cried King Loc, rubbing his hands.

And having embraced the old Nur, he went out of the well in peals of laughter.

All along the road he held his sides to laugh at his ease; his head wagged with mirth; his beard rose and fell on his chest; "ha! ha! ha! ha! ha! ha! ha!" The little men who met him also began to laugh like him, out of sympathy. Seeing them laugh, others laughed too; this laughter spread from one to another till the whole inside of the earth was shaken with a jovial great guffaw.

CHAPTER XVI

TELLS THE MARVELLOUS ADVENTURE
OF GEORGE OF THE WHITE MOOR

King Loc did not laugh long; on the contrary, he hid the face of a very unhappy little man under his bedclothes. Thinking of George of the White Moor, prisoner of the Sylphs, he could not sleep the whole night. So, at that hour of the morning when the dwarfs who have a dairymaid for a friend go to milk the cows in her place while she sleeps like a log in her white bed, little King Loc revisited Nur in his deep well.

"Nur," he said to him, "you did not tell me what he was doing among the Sylphs."

The old Nur thought that King Loc had gone out of his mind, and he was not very frightened, because he was certain that King Loc, if he became mad, would certainly turn into a graceful, witty, amiable, and kindly madman. The madness of the dwarfs is gentle like their sanity and delightfully fantastic. But King Loc was not mad; at least he was not more so than lovers usually are.

"I mean George of the White Moor," he said to the old man, who had forgotten this young man as completely as possible.

Then the learned Nur arranged the lenses and the mirrors in a careful pattern, but so intricate that it had the appearance of disorder, and showed to King Loc in the mirror the very shape of George of the White Moor, such as he was when the Sylphs carried him off. By properly choosing and skilfully directing the instruments, the dwarf showed the lovelorn king the whole adventure of the son of that countess who was warned of her end by a white rose. And here expressed in words is what the two little men saw in the reality of form and colour.

When George was carried away in the icy arms of the daughter of the lake, he felt the water press his eyes and his breast, and he thought it was death. Yet he heard songs that were like caresses, and he was steeped in a delicious coolness. When he opened his eyes again he found himself in a grotto; it had crystal pillars in which the delicate tints of the rainbow shone. At the end of this grotto there was a large shell of mother-of-pearl, irisated with the softest colours: it was a canopy spreading over a throne of coral and weeds where sat the queen of the Sylphs. But the aspect of the sovereign of the waters had lights softer than the sheen of mother-of-pearl and of crystal. She smiled at the child brought to her by her women and let her green eyes rest on him long.

"Friend," she at length said to him, "welcome in our world, where you will be spared every pain. For you, no dry books or rough exercises, nothing coarse that recalls the earth and its labours, but only the songs, the dances, and the friendship of the Sylphs."

So the blue-haired women taught the child music, waltzing, and a thousand amusements. They loved to bind on his forehead the shells that starred their own locks. But he, thinking of his country, gnawed his fists in impatience.

The years went by, and George's wish to see the earth again was unchanged and fervent, the hardy earth burnt by the sun, frozen by the snow, the native earth of sufferings and affections, the earth where he had seen, where he wished to see Bee again. Now he was growing into a big boy, and a slight golden down ran along his upper lip. Boldness came to him with his beard, and one day he appeared before the queen of the Sylphs, and having bowed, said to her:

"My lady, I have come, if you deign to permit it, to take leave of you. I am going back to the Clarides."

"Dear friend," the queen answered, smiling, "I cannot grant you the leave you demand, for I keep you in my crystal manor to make you my friend."

"My lady," George replied, "I feel unworthy of so great an honour."

"This is the effect of your courtesy. No good knight ever thinks he has done enough to win the love of his lady. Further, you are yet too young to know all your merits. Be sure, dear friend, that nobody wishes you anything but good. You only have to obey your lady."

"My lady, I love Bee of the Clarides, and I will love no other lady but her."

The queen, very pale, but still more beautiful, cried:

"A mortal woman, a gross daughter of men, this Bee, how can you love that?"

"I do not know, but I know that I love her."

"Very well, you will recover."

And she detained the young man in the delights of the crystal manor.

He did not know what a woman was, and was more like Achilles among the daughters of Lycomedes than Tannhauser in the magic mountain. So he wandered gloomily along the walls of the immense palace, looking for an opening to run away; but on all sides he saw the floods enclosing his luminous prison in their mute and magnificent kingdom. Through the transparent walls he watched the anemones bloom and the coral flowering, while purple, azure, and golden fish sparkled and sported above the delicate madrepores and the glistening shells. These marvels did not interest him; but lulled by the delicious songs of the Sylphs, he slowly felt his will give way, and his whole soul dissolve.

He was all slackness and indifference, when he found by chance in a gallery of the palace an old worn book of vellum, studded with copper nails. The book, found in a wreck at the bottom of the sea, dealt with chivalry and ladies, and there were told at length stories of the adventures of heroes who went through the world fighting giants, redressing wrongs, protecting widows, and assisting orphans for the love of justice and the honour of beauty. George flushed and grew pale in turn with admiration, shame, and anger at the tale of these splendid adventures. He could not contain himself:

"I also," he cried, "will be a good knight! I also will go through the world punishing the wicked and helping the unhappy for the good of men and the name of my lady Bee."

Then his heart grew great with courage. He strode with drawn sword through the crystal mansions. The white women fled and vanished before him like the silvery waves of a lake. Their queen alone saw him come upon her unmoved. She fixed on him the cold look of her green eyes.

He rushes to her; he cries:

"Unclasp the charm which you have thrown on me. Open me the road to earth. I wish to fight in the sun like a knight. I wish to return to love, to suffer, and to struggle. Give me back the true life and the true light. Give me action and achievement; if you do not I will kill you, wicked woman!"

She shook her head smiling, to say "no." She was beautiful and calm. George struck her with all his strength. But his sword broke against the glittering bosom of the queen of the Sylphs.

"Child!" she said.

And she had him shut up in a kind of crystal funnel which formed a cell under the manor; round it sharks prowled, opening their monstrous jaws armed with a triple row of sharp teeth. And it seemed as if at each charge they must break the thin partition of glass; it was not possible to sleep in this strange cell.

The point of this submarine funnel rested on a rocky bottom which was the dome of the furthest and the least known cavern of the Empire of the dwarfs.

This is what the two little men saw in the course of an hour as exactly as if they had followed George all the days of his life. The ancient Nur, after having displayed the cell scene in all its sadness, spoke to King Loc much in the way of a showman when he has shown the magic lantern to little children.

"King Loc," he said to him, "I have shown you all you wished to see, and, your knowledge being perfect, I can add nothing to it. I am not anxious to know whether what you have seen has pleased you; it is enough that it is true. Science takes no account of pleasing or displeasing. It is inhuman. It is not science, it is poetry which charms and consoles. That is why poetry is more necessary than science. King Loc, go and compose a song."

King Loc went out of the well without speaking a word.

CHAPTER XVII

IN WHICH KING LOC MAKES A TERRIBLE JOURNEY

On leaving the well of science King Loc went to his treasure, took a ring from a box of which he alone had a key, and put it on his finger. The bezel of this ring shone brightly, for it was made of magic stone whose virtues will be discovered in the course of this story. King Loc then went to his palace, where he put on a travelling cloak, drew on heavy boots, and took a stick. Then he set out through the crowded street, the broad roads, the villages, and the halls of porphyry, the lakes of petroleum, and the grottos of crystal which communicated with each other by narrow openings.

He seemed pensive and spoke words which had no sense. But he walked on steadily. Mountains blocked the way and he climbed the mountains; cliffs yawned at his feet and he went down the cliffs; he crossed fords, he passed through grisly regions darkened by the fumes of sulphur. He walked over burning lava, in which his feet printed themselves; he seemed to be an extremely determined traveller. He entered dark caverns where the sea water, trickling in drops, fell like tears along the weeds and made pools in the uneven soil in which innumerable crustaceans grew monstrously. Enormous crabs, giant crayfish, spiders of the sea, cracked under the feet of the dwarf and made off, leaving behind a claw, and waking in their flight hideous hoary cuttle-fish, who suddenly waved their hundred arms and spat from their beaks a reeking poison. King Loc went on all the same. He reached the end of these caverns staggering under a load of monsters armed with stings, double jagged pincers, claws that curled up to his neck, and sullen eyes brandished at the end of long branches. He climbed the side of the cavern clinging to the roughnesses of the rock, and the armoured beasts went up with him, and he only stopped when by groping he found a stone that jutted out of the vaulted summit. With his magic ring he touched this stone, which immediately fell with a great crash, and immediately a flood of light poured its lovely streams into the cavern and put to flight the beasts bred in darkness.

King Loc put his head through the opening where the light came from, saw George of the White Moor thinking of Bee and the earth, and mourning in his glass prison. For King Loc had made this subterranean journey to release the prisoner of the Sylphs. But seeing this big head, all hair, eyebrows, and beard, look at him from the bottom of the crystal funnel, George thought a great danger threatened him, and he felt for the sword at his side, forgetting he had broken it on the bosom of the green-eyed woman. Meanwhile King Loc examined him curiously.

"Pooh!" he said to himself, "it is only a child."

Certainly it was a very simple child, and he owed to his great simplicity his escape from the delicious and mortal kisses of the queen of the Sylphs. Aristotle with all his learning could not have got out of it so easily.

George, seeing himself defenceless, said:

"What do you want of me, big head? Why hurt me, if I have never hurt you?"

King Loc answered in a jovial and gruff tone:

"My dear boy, you do not know if you have hurt me, for you are ignorant of effect and cause, of reflex action, and generally of all philosophy. But do not let us talk of this. If you are not reluctant to leave your funnel, come through here."

George immediately insinuated himself into the cavern, slid down the wall, and, as soon as he reached the bottom:

"You are a good little man," he said to his deliverer, "I will like you all my life; but do you know where Bee of the Clarides is?"

"I know a great many things," answered the dwarf, "and especially that I do not like inquisitive people."

George, hearing these words, remained quite abashed, and he silently followed his guide through the thick and murky air where cuttlefish and crabs were moving. Then King Loc said to him with a grin:

"The road is rather rough, my young prince."

"Sir," George answered him, "the way to freedom is always pleasant, and I am not afraid of being lost by following my benefactor."

Little King Loc bit his lips. When he reached the hall of porphyry, he showed the young man a staircase made in the stone by which the dwarfs go up above ground.

"Here is your road," he said to him, "good-bye."

"Do not say good-bye," replied George, "tell me you will see me again. My life belongs to you after what you have done for me."

King Loc answered:

"What I have done was not for you, but for another. We had better not see each other again, because we might not like each other."

George replied unaffectedly and seriously:

"I did not think that my release would give me pain. And yet it has. Good-bye, sir."

"I wish you a good journey," King Loc cried roughly.

Now this staircase ended in a lonely quarry which lay less than a league from the castle of the Clarides.

King Loc pursued his way muttering:

"This boy has neither the learning nor the wealth of the dwarfs. I do not really know why he is loved by Bee, unless it is that he is young, handsome, loyal, and bold."

He returned to the town laughing to himself like a man who has played a practical joke on some one. Passing in front of Bee's house, he pushed his big head through the window, as he had done into the glass funnel, and he saw the young girl embroidering a veil with silver flowers.

"Rejoice, Bee," he said to her.

"And you," she answered, "little King Loc, may you never have anything to wish for, or at least anything to regret."

There was something he wished for, but really he had nothing to regret. This thought gave him a large appetite for supper. After eating a great number of truffled pheasants, he called Bob.

"Bob," he said to him, "get on your crow: go to the Princess of the Dwarfs and tell her that George of the White Moor, who was for a long time a prisoner of the Sylphs, returned to-day to the Clarides."

He spoke, and Bob flew off on his crow.

CHAPTER XVIII

TELLS THE MARVELLOUS MEETING THAT OCCURRED TO JOHN, THE MASTER TAILOR, AND OF THE GOOD SONG SUNG BY THE BIRDS OF THE GROVE TO THE DUCHESS

When George found himself on the earth where he was born, the first person he met was John, the old master tailor, carrying on his arm a scarlet suit for the steward of the castle. The old fellow gave a great cry at the sight of the young lord.

"St. James!" he said, "if it is not his Highness George of the White Moor, who was drowned in the lake seven years ago, then it is his ghost or the devil himself!"

"It is not a ghost or a devil, my good John, but it is that George of the White Moor who used to slip into your shop and ask you for little bits of cloth to make dresses for the dolls of my sister Bee."

But the old fellow exclaimed:

"So you were not drowned, your Highness? I am very pleased. You look quite well. My grandson, Peter, who used to climb up into my arms of a Sunday morning to see you go by on horseback next to the Duchess, has become a good workman and a fine, handsome lad. He will be glad to know you are not at the bottom of the water, and that the fish have not eaten you as he thought. He is accustomed to say about this the most amusing things in the world; for he is full of wit, your Highness. And it is a fact that everybody regrets you in the Clarides. You were such a promising little boy. I will remember to my last day how once you asked me for my needle, and as I would not give it to you, because you were not old enough to handle it without danger, you answered me that you would go into the wood and pick the fine needles of the pines. This is what you said, and it still makes me laugh. Upon my word this is what you said. Our little Peter used also to make excellent answers. He is a cooper at present, at your service, your Highness."

"I will employ none other but him. But, Master John, give me some news of Bee and the Duchess."

"Alas, where have you been, your Highness, not to know that Princess Bee was carried off, seven years ago, by the dwarfs of the mountain? She disappeared the very day you were drowned; and it can be said that on that day the Clarides lost their two sweetest flowers. The Duchess has mourned greatly ever since. This always makes me say that the great people of this world have their trouble like the poorest workmen, and this is a sign that we are all children of Adam. Accordingly a cat may look at a king, as they say. By the same token the good Duchess saw her hair grow grey and lost all her gaiety. And when, in the spring, she walks about in a black dress under the grove where the birds sing, the smallest of these birds is more enviable than the sovereign of the Clarides. Her sorrow, however, is not hope-less, your Highness; for, if she has no news of you, at least she knows by dreams that her daughter Bee is alive."

Old John said these things and many others, too; but George was not listening to him since he had heard that Bee was a pris-oner of the dwarfs.

He reflected:

"The dwarfs detain Bee under the earth; a dwarf got me out of my crystal prison. These little men have not all the same habits; my deliverer surely does not belong to the tribe of those who carried off my sister."

He did not know what to think, unless it was that Bee must be released.

Now they were going through the town, and, as they passed, the old women standing at their thresholds asked each other who this young stranger was, and they agreed his appearance was handsome. The more wary, having recognised the Lord of the White Moor, thought they saw a ghost, and fled, crossing themselves vigorously.

"Holy water ought to be cast at him," said an old woman, "and he would vanish leaving a disgusting smell of sulphur. He is carrying off Master John, the tailor, and quite certainly he will plunge him all alive into the flames of hell."

"Gently, old woman," a burgess replied, "the young lord is alive and a good deal more so than you and me. He is as fresh as a rose, and rather seems to have come from some noble court than from the other world. Men come back from far, my good woman; witness the squire Freeheart, who came back to us from Rome last Candlemas."

And Mary, the armourer's daughter, having admired George, went up to her maiden room, and kneeling then before the image of the Holy Virgin: "Holy Virgin," she said, "grant me a husband like this young lord."

Every one spoke in their own way of the return of George, so much so that the news flew from mouth to mouth to the ears of the Duchess, who was then walking in the orchard. Her heart beat high, and she heard all the birds in the grove sing:

Teewhit, teewhit, teewhit,
Teewhit, teewhit, teewhit,
George of the White Moor,
Teewhit, teewhit, teewhit,
Whom you brought up,
Teewhit, teewhit, teewhit,
Is here, here, here, here.

Freeheart respectfully approached her, and said to her:

"Your Grace, George of the White Moor, whom you thought to be dead, has returned. I am going to make a song about it."

Still the birds sang:

Teewhit, teewhit, twit, twit,
Is here, here, here,
Is here, here, here.

And when she saw the child coming she had brought up as a son she opened her arms and fell in a swoon.

CHAPTER XIX

TELLS OF A LITTLE SATIN SLIPPER

People were pretty certain in the Clarides that Bee had been carried off by the dwarfs. It was also the belief of the Duchess; but her dreams did not give her any exact information.

"We will find her," said George.

"We will find her," answered Freeheart.

"And we will bring her back to her mother," said George.

"And we will bring her back," answered Freeheart.

"And we will marry her," said George.

"And we will marry her," answered Freeheart.

And they inquired among the inhabitants concerning the habits of the dwarfs and the mysterious facts of Bee's capture.

This led them to question the nurse Glauce, who had been the nurse of the Duchess of the Clarides; but now Glauce was old and fed the fowls in her farmyard.

There the squire and his master found her. She was crying "Ss! ss! ss! chick! chick! chick; ss! ss! ss! ss!" and throwing grain to the chicks.

"Ss! ss! ss! chick! chick! chick! It is your Highness! Ss! ss! ss! Is it possible that you have become so big…ss! and so handsome? Ss! ss! shoo! shoo! shoo! Do you see that big one there eating the share of the small ones? Shoo! shoo! So it is everywhere in the world, your Highness. All the good goes to the rich. The lean get leaner, while the fat get fatter. For there is no justice on this earth. What can I do for you, your Highness? You will surely each of you take a glass of ale?"

"We will take one with pleasure, Glauce, and I will kiss you because you nursed the mother of her whom I love best in the world."

"It is quite true, your Highness; my baby had its first tooth in six months and fourteen days, and on that occasion the late Duchess made me a present. It is quite true."

"Well, tell us, Glauce, what you know of the dwarfs who carried off Bee."

"Alas! your Highness, I know nothing of the dwarfs who carried her off. And how can an old woman like me know anything? I forgot the little I ever learnt long ago, and I have not even enough memory to remember where I put my spectacles. I often look for them when I have them on. Try this ale, it is nice and cool."

"Your health, Glauce; but I am told your husband knew something about Bee's carrying off."

"It is quite true, your Highness. Though he had never got any education, he knew a great many things that he learnt in inns and taverns. He never forgot anything. If he was still in this world and sitting at this table with us, he could tell you stories by the week. He told me so many and so many of all kinds that they have made a muddle inside my head, and I cannot, at this moment, make head or tail of any of them. It is quite true, your Highness."

Yes, it is quite true, and the head of the old nurse was as useless as an old cracked kettle. George and Freeheart had all the trouble in the world to get any good out of her. At last, by sifting her, they drew out a story which began in this style:

"Seven years ago, your Highness, on the very day you and Bee got into the scrape from which neither of you came back, my late husband went into the hills to sell a horse. It is quite true. He gave his beast a good feed of oats with a dash of cider in it, so that it might have a firm leg and a bright eye; he took it to the market near the hills. His corn and his cider were not lost, for it made his horse sell better. It is the same with beasts as with men; they are judged by appearances. My late husband was pleased at the good business he had done; he offered to drink with his friends, undertaking to drink fair to them. And

I must tell you, your Highness, that there was not a man in the whole Clarides who could drink fairer with his friends than my husband. So much so that, on this day, after a great deal of good feeling and harmony, he came back alone in the twilight and took a wrong road, for want of finding the right one. Finding himself near a cavern, he saw as clear as it was possible in his condition and at that hour a band of little men carrying a boy or a girl on a stretcher. He ran away for fear of a mishap, for wine did not deprive him of discretion. But at some distance from the cavern, having let his pipe fall, he bent to pick it up and took hold of a little satin slipper instead. He made a remark about it which he liked to repeat when he was in a good temper. 'This is the first time,' he said to himself, 'that a pipe changes into a slipper.' Now, as this slipper was the slipper of a little girl, he thought that she who had lost it in the wood had been carried off by the dwarfs, and that it was her capture he had seen. He was just on the point of putting the slipper in his pocket when little men, covered with hoods, threw themselves upon him and gave him so many smacks on the head that he remained on the spot quite dazed."

"Glauce! Glauce!" cried George, "it is Bee's slipper! Give it me that I may kiss it a thousand times. It shall lie on my heart for ever, in a bag of scented silk, and when I die it shall be put in my coffin."

"As you please, your Highness; but where will you go to get it? The dwarfs took it back from my poor husband, and he even thought that why he had been so thoroughly beaten was because he tried to put it in his pocket to show the magistrates. He was accustomed to say on the subject when he was in a good temper…"

"Enough! Enough! Only tell me the name of the cave."

"My lord, it is called the cave of the dwarfs, and it is well called so. My late husband…"

"Glauce! not a word more! But you, Freeheart, do you know where this cave is?"

"My lord," answered Freeheart, finishing his mug of ale, "you would be quite certain I do if you knew my songs better. I have composed at least a dozen on this cave, and I have described it without forgetting the smallest sprig of moss. I venture to say, my lord, that of these twelve songs, six are really worth something. But the six others are not to be disdained. I will just sing you one or two…"

"Freeheart," cried George, "we will seize the cave of the dwarfs, and we will deliver Bee!"

"Nothing could be more certain," answered Freeheart.

CHAPTER XX

IN WHICH A DANGEROUS ADVENTURE IS RELATED

As soon as night came, and the whole castle was asleep, George and Freeheart slipped into the low hall to get arms. There, under the smoky joists, gleamed lances, swords, dirks, espadons, hunting knives, daggers, all that is required to kill man and wolf. Under each rafter, a complete suit of armour stood upright, holding itself so sternly and proudly that it seemed as if it was still filled by the soul of the brave man who had arrayed himself in it in bygone days to go on great adventures. And the glove clasped the lance in ten iron fingers, while the shield rested on the tassets of the thigh, as if to teach that prudence is necessary to courage and that the good soldier is armed for defence as well as for attack. George selected amid so ample a choice the suit of armour which the father of Bee had carried as far as the isles of Avalon and of Thule. He put it on with the help of Freeheart, and he did not forget the shield on which was blazoned proper the golden sun of the Clarides. Freeheart, on the other hand, arrayed himself in the good old steel coat of his grandfather and crowned himself with an obsolete headpiece, to which he added a kind of moth-eaten and ragged plume, feather, or brush. He made this choice for fun and to look comical; for he considered that gaiety, good at all hours, is especially useful when there are great dangers to be incurred.

Having thus armed themselves, they went off, under the moon, over the dark fields. Freeheart had tied the horses at the edge of a little wood, near the fortress gate, where they found them gnawing the bark of the bushes; these horses were very swift, and it took them less than an hour to reach, amid dancing will o' wisps and confused visions, the mountains of the dwarfs.

"Here is the cave," said Freeheart.

The lord and squire dismounted. Sword in hand, they entered the cave. Great courage was required to engage in such an adventure. But George was in love and Freeheart was faithful. And as the most delightful of poets says:

"What cannot Friendship do guided by sweet Love?"

The lord and the squire walked in the darkness for nearly an hour; then they saw a great blaze, at which they were astonished. It was one of those meteors with which we know the dwarfs illuminate their kingdom.

By the light of this subterranean brightness they saw they were at the base of an ancient castle.

"Here," said George, "is the castle which we must seize."

"Certainly," answered Freeheart, "but allow me to drink a few drops of this wine which I brought with me as a weapon, for a good wine makes a good man, and a good man makes a good spear, and a good spear makes a bad foe."

George, not seeing a living soul, roughly struck with the hilt of his sword the door of the castle. A small quavering voice made him lift his head, and he saw at one of the windows a very small old man with a long beard who asked him:

"Who are you?"

"George of the White Moor."

"And what do you want?"

"I want to take back Bee of the Clarides, whom you unjustly detain in your mole-hill, ugly moles that you are!"

The dwarf disappeared, and again George found himself alone with Freeheart, who said to him:

"My lord, I do not know if I am guilty of exaggeration when I state that in your answer to the dwarf you did not perhaps exhaust all the resources of the most persuasive eloquence."

Freeheart feared nothing, but he was old. His manners, like the top of his head, had been smoothed by time, and he did not like to see people annoyed. George, on the other hand, rushed about yelling:

"Vile earthmen, moles, badgers, dormice, ferrets, and water-rats, only open the door and I will cut all your ears off."

But hardly had he finished speaking these words when the bronze door of the castle opened of itself. No one could be seen pushing the huge leaves.

George was frightened, and yet he stepped through the mysterious door because his courage was greater than his fear. Once inside the court, he saw at all the windows, in all the galleries, on all the roofs, on all the gables, inside the lamp and even on the chimney-pots dwarfs armed with bows and cross-bows.

He heard the bronze door shut behind him, and a shower of arrows began to fall hard on his head and his shoulders. For the second time he was very frightened, and for the second time he overcame his fear.

Shield on arm, and sword in hand, he went up the stairs, when suddenly he saw, standing on the highest step, and calmly majestic, a stately dwarf, bearing the golden sceptre, the royal crown, and the purple mantle. And this dwarf he recognised to be the little man who had freed him from his glass prison. Then he threw himself at his feet and said to him in tears:

"My benefactor, is it you? Are you one of those who have taken from me Bee whom I love?"

"I am King Loc," answered the dwarf. "I have kept Bee with me to teach her the secrets of the dwarfs. Child, you have come upon my kingdom like hail on a garden of flowers. But the dwarfs, less weak than men, do not grow irritated as they do. I am too much above you in mind to feel anger at your acts, whatever they may be. Of all the advantages I have over you there is one that I will carefully keep; it is that of being just. I will send for Bee, and I will ask her if she wishes to follow you. I will do this not because you demand it, but because it is my duty."

There was a deep silence, and Bee appeared in a white dress with her fair hair loose. As soon as she saw George she ran to throw herself in his arms, and clasped with all her might the iron breast of the knight.

Then King Loc said to her:

"Bee, is it true that this is the man whom you wish to marry?"

"It is true, very true, that this is the man, little King Loc," answered Bee. "Look, little men, how I laugh and how I am happy."

And she began to cry. Her tears fell on George's cheek, and they were tears of happiness; laughter mingled with the tears and a thousand delightful words which had no sense, like those murmured by little children. She did not reflect that the sight of her happiness could sadden the heart of King Loc.

"Dearest," George said to her, "I find you again just as I wished you to be: the most beautiful and the best of beings. You love me! Heaven be thanked, you love me! But, Bee, do you not also love King Loc a little, who drew me from the glass prison where the Sylphs kept me far from you?"

Bee turned to King Loc:

"Little King Loc, you did this!" she cried: "you loved me and you freed the one who loved me and whom I loved..."

She could say no more, and she fell on her knees, her head in her hands.

All the little men, witnesses of this scene, shed tears on their crossbows. King Loc alone kept an unmoved face. Bee, discovering in him so much magnanimity and so much kindness, felt for him the love of a daughter for a father. She seized the hand of her lover and said:

"George, I love you: heaven only knows how much I love you. But how can I leave little King Loc?"

"Ha, ha! you are both prisoners of mine," cried King Loc in a terrible voice.

He put on a terrible voice by way of amusement and to play a good joke. But really he was not angry. Freeheart came to him and bent a knee to the ground.

"Sir," he said, "will your Highness be pleased to let me share the captivity of the master I serve?"

Bee, recognising him, said to him:

"It is you, my good Freeheart. I am pleased to see you again. You are wearing a very ugly feather. Tell me, have you composed any new songs?"

And King Loc took them all three off to dinner.

CHAPTER XXI

IN WHICH ALL ENDS WELL

The next day George and Freeheart dressed themselves in sumptuous clothes which the dwarfs had prepared for them, and betook themselves to the Hall of State where King Loc, in the dress of an Emperor, soon came to join them as he had promised. He was followed by his officers wearing arms, and furs of a wild magnificence, and helmets on which swan-wings waved. The dwarfs, thronging in crowds, came in by the windows, the ventilators, and the chimneys, and even crept under the seats.

King Loc got up on a stone table, at the end of which were drawn up rows of flagons, candlesticks, bowls, and cups of fine gold and of marvellous workmanship. He motioned to Bee and to George to come near, and said:

"Bee, a law of the Dwarf people requires that a stranger received within our house should be free at the end of seven full years. You have spent seven years in our midst, Bee, and I would be a bad citizen and a guilty king if I detained you longer. But before I let you go away, I wish, not having been able to marry you, to betroth you myself to the man you have chosen. I do so with joy, because I love you more than myself, and my pain, if any is left, is like a little shadow unnoticed in my happiness. Bee of the Clarides, Princess of the Dwarfs, give me your hand; and you, George of the White Moor, give me yours."

Having put the hand of George in that of Bee, King Loc turned to his people and said in a loud voice:

"Little men, my children, you are witnesses that these two here undertake mutually to marry each other on earth. Let them return there together and together bring forth deeds of courage, modesty, and faithfulness, as good gardeners tend and bring to flower roses, carnations and peonies."

At these words the dwarfs shouted loudly, and, not knowing whether they ought to lament or to rejoice, they were distracted by contrary feelings. King Loc turned again to the two betrothed, and showing them the bowls, the flagons, all the splendid plate:

"These," he said, "are the presents of the dwarfs. Take them, Bee, they will recall your little friends; they are given by them and not by me. You will know in a moment what I mean to give you."

There was a long silence. King Loc gazed with a lovely look of tenderness at Bee, whose beautiful radiant head, crowned with roses, rested on the shoulder of her betrothed.

Then he spoke again in these terms:

"Children, it is not enough to love much; you must love well. Great love is good, undoubtedly; wise love is better. May yours be as mild as it is strong; may it want nothing, not even indulgence, and may some pity be mingled with it. You are young, beautiful and good; but you are human, and, for that very reason, subject to many miseries. This is why, if some pity does not form part of the feelings you have for each other, these feelings will not be adapted to the circumstances of your common life; they will be like holiday clothes which are no protection against the wind and the rain. You only love those securely whom you love even in their weaknesses and meannesses. Mercy, forgiveness, consolation, that is love and all its science."

King Loc stopped, overcome by sweet and powerful emotions. He resumed his speech:

"Children, be happy. Keep your happiness, keep it carefully."

While he spoke, Pic, Tad, Dic, Bob, Truc, and Paw, clinging to Bee's white mantle, covered with kisses the girl's naked arms and hands. And they begged her not to leave them. Then King Loc drew from his belt a ring, the stone of which flung showers of light. It was the magic ring with which he had opened the dungeon of the Sylphs. He slipped Bee's finger through it, and said:

"Bee, receive at my hands this ring, which will allow you to enter at all times, you and your husband, the kingdom of the dwarfs. You will be received with delight and helped in every way. On the other hand, teach the children you will have not to despise the innocent and industrious little men who live under the earth."

NOTES

Chapter I.

Now that we know all about Princess Bee, we may find it pleasant to look backward and think a little about the story, chapter by chapter, to find out whether it has come to stay in our minds. Some stories do and others don't. We are glad to forget some stories, but I do not think that the story of Bee is one of that kind. Besides, it is told with such loving carefulness that, for the sake of the writer, who wrote that he might please and inspire us, we ought to read it again with a quiet mind, undisturbed by any thought of what is going to happen next; for now we know all about that.

It is a story of that wonder time so often spoken of as "long, long ago," and its date does not matter; but you will see from the first chapter that it belongs to the time of the knights, the best of whom tried to remedy things that were wrong and make the world a finer place in which to live.

Do you like the Countess of the White Moor? And why? How much older was George than Bee?

Chapter II.

Read over several times the description of the estates of the Duchess of Clarides (there are three bites to this cherry). It is such a good "pen-picture" and there are many more in this story for which you ought to watch with care. The old monk in the tower with his birds and his books is worth thinking about and so are his rules; so also are the rules of the Duchess. There is a good "pen-picture" with two trees and two children in it. I wonder if you could sketch it?

Chapter III.

Do they teach falconry in your school? If not, you might at least try to find out something about it, for it was a fascinating sport—except, of course, for the little birds—much better fun than learning several styles of handwriting or getting "grammatical instruction with barbarous terminology." What a lovely jumble of big words! What about that sentence, "affectionate lessons are the only good lessons"? And whatever is "inebriety "? It must be something very dreadful. I fancy it is something catching and can most easily be caught at "Tin-jugs," and "Red Lions," and "Indian Queens," and "Bull and Bushes," and such-like places where they know absolutely nothing about synecdoche or aposiopesis either.

Chapter IV.

There are some lovely colours in the first bit of this chapter. Perhaps you could get someone to make a colour-sketch? And pearls have a "mild splendour," haven't they, quite different from diamonds or rubies? If you are a girl wouldn't you like to have a hair-ribbon like Bee's? George and Bee were taught a beautiful lesson that morning, and learnt it, too. I wish we could all describe beautiful scenery as beautifully as the Duchess could—and, by-the-way, look carefully at the iris flower when you meet with one again. Sylphs? Have you another name for them? What a sounding title the old beggar-woman gave herself, and what a well furnished kitchen she had! Have you a pipkin and a caldron at home? What are the duties of Dwarfs?

Chapter V.

Have you ever noticed that hills and woods are really "blue in the distance"? A great many writers have done so. What a charming definition (horrid word) Princess Bee gave of the horizon, and how differently she thought of the bigness of the world from George. Do you think they would find lobsters by fishing under the old stone bridge? (Perhaps, however, this is too severe a question for a tale about "long, long ago.") Those forbidden Sylphs were still in the children's minds, but Bee had less fear than George—or was she daring George to go? Which of the two children was the best quarreller?

Chapter VI.

And now, who is the brave adventurer? There is a pretty picture of which the "Headless Woman" is the centre. Read the description again and again and look at the picture with closed eyes. There is another with Bee in the centre, holding out her skirt for the cherries. Bee's teachers had not taught her economics, had they? It would be hard to find a more charming description of a walk than is contained in this chapter. Bee is soon plunged in despair, but George is a little Greatheart and soon has his reward. Read slowly and more than once the description of the lake. The sudden appearance of the goose-girl gives us another pretty picture. What is a demijohn? How does Bee tell us that the day is waning? Consider the words "Reeds, like pliant swords," and the pretty coloured flower-picture at the end of the chapter.

Chapter VII.

George still plays the part of Greatheart manfully and is ready for any event, having used his observing powers on the fruits and berries like a Boy Scout. Think of that sharp picture against the pale sky of evening—"a little dwarf riding on a crow." Then of the changing picture—like a lovely scene in a play—as night falls upon the lake. See how the Sylphs come while the boy stands entranced. Did he remember the words of Bee's mother as he was carried "through the waters, in halls of crystal and porphyry"? And what a lovely word the last one is!

Chapter VIII.

It would be good fun to try to draw a dwarf from the description given at the beginning of this chapter, helped by a glance at some of the little pictures in this book. Can't you feel how quick the dwarfs were as you say the words "incredible nimbleness," rolling them round your tongue? I wonder what it means to "look like an old poet." Pic's last sentence, at all events, is very like poetry. Rug is very good at argument and at sticking to his own opinion. Tad is a dwarf of character—"Justice should prevail, and not custom." As for Pan, he might have been a very sensible father, mightn't he? There is a pretty picture when Bee raises herself upon her elbow and another one of a different kind when Pic stands upon his dignity (to make himself taller) and speaks the sounding sentence which begins, "She is only a child." And what a depth of real truth there is in Tad's words, "You will consider us less ugly when you like us better." No one who is loved can be ugly to the one who loves.

And what a sad reproach there is in Tad's words to Rug: "You are more like a man than a dwarf." This chapter ends with another charming picture.

Chapter IX.

How many colours or tints are mentioned in the first paragraph of this chapter? In the next paragraph poetry and gentle fun have kissed each other. A dwarf of "great majesty"? Oh, yes. Majesty is not a matter of inches. The dwarf monarch understood little girls in a wonderful way and Bee was soon at her ease as every guest is who asks for a pair of slippers, right off. The next thing such a guest would do would be to poke the fire! The illustrious Belisarius? He was a famous general who won many victories in Italy and the East, and was brave, generous, just and faithful and afraid of nothing but his wife. Bee was just a little ungracious about those slippers, don't you think? But there was some excuse for her—she did want to be at home again. It would be a lovely arrangement if those who love each other could exchange dreams when they are parted for a time. Some people say they do, and possibly the dwarf poet believed it to be possible.

Chapter X.

It was a strange but beautiful underground world in which the dwarfs had their home. Why lava pavement? Bee's lessons must have been fascinating. If only we could all learn without books! Then perhaps we also should "move with grace and express ourselves according to the rule of poetry." What a delightful picture of a puppet show is given in this chapter! There are clever men and women to-day who can make dolls act in this way. Read the description again, for it is well worth while. Wouldn't you like to play the theorbo? It has a lovely name. Did the dwarfs change as the days and months passed and the years made their round?

Chapters XI. and XII.

The deep, deep darkness between the rocky walls makes the light shine all the brighter, and Bee's exclamation might be that of a blind girl whose sight is suddenly restored. Have you ever seen a chalice, a pyx, or a patin, and would you know them if you saw them again? Or a thurible? And wouldn't you like that set of moonstone chessmen? What a wonderful description of a coffer full of jewels! Yet, with all this wealth before her Bee chooses to go back to earth and into the sunshine back to her mother and George of the White Moor, more precious than pearls. Read again and again, nay, learn by heart what King Loc said to Bee after he had tested her—for he was only testing her all the time. Was there ever such a proposal of marriage? But little King Loc has his own dignity—also his hopes.

Chapter XIII.

Who would be a princess and wear a crown which interfered with flowing locks and merry gambols? The story-teller strikes a sad note. Bee and the little king are both unhappy and there is a pathetic and very beautiful picture of the princess gazing on the sunbeam; another of her arrival on earth again. The king's instructions are difficult and there is danger in them. The journey home is fascinating, reminding us of Peter and Wendy on the way to the Land of Lost Boys; so also is the arrival home, which is fully described. But the sad ending is told in a few curt words. It is much too pitiful for a long description.

Chapter XIV.

Is this story beginning to remind you of an old, old tale told long ago among the Ancient Greeks, a tale of a lost princess carried off to the Underworld by Pluto and mourned on earth by Ceres, the goddess of the corn? If you happen to know that old, old story you will be able to make interesting comparisons. But to return to King Loc. The secret comes out. Did Bee know that she loved George of the White Moor when King Loc had asked her, long before, whether she loved anyone else? Have you known Bee's secret all along? The effect of her declaration is rather piteous—with a smile behind the sadness. King Loc's exit is very dignified and dramatic and, by the way, what an excellent play could be made from this story, or a series of tableaux.

Chapter XV.

Poor King Loc cannot understand the situation. He is a king, he has learning, wealth, and merit. Why; therefore, does not Bee love him? Further, he is good and wishes to be just. Poor little King Loc! Nur introduces and describes himself in a speech worth learning and remembering. His long speech about ourselves is full of wisdom and warning. Read it again and again. The last portion is very beautiful. And what a wonderful way the dwarfs had of finding things out without books. George of the Moor was easily traced. King Loc is very undwarflike or, let us say, very human when he learns where George is. But would the laugh of these little creatures even in unison be a "jovial great guffaw"? Surely it is only jolly giants who make great guffaws. Perhaps you can describe the dwarf laughter in a better way. What do you think the writer means by making Nur live in a deep well?

Chapter XVI.

There is an interesting glimpse of one of the duties of the dwarfs in the first paragraph of this chapter. Have you read Mrs. Ewing's Lob-lie-by-the-Fire? If not, get it from the library and read about what one of our poets calls "the lubber-fiend." Dwarf madness seems to be an amiable thing. "A shell of mother-of-pearl irisated." Remember that Iris was the Greek goddess of the rainbow. George was no more happy among the beauties of the sea-world than was Bee among the treasures of the caves, and he learnt the same lesson as she did. You will find it in the sentence which begins: "The years went by." Compare King Loc with the Princess of the Sylphs. Achilles was the Greek hero who fought against Troy and killed their champion, Hector. Disguised as a girl, he was once sent by his mother to the court of King Lycomedes because she wished to prevent his setting out for the Siege of Troy. Tannhauser is the hero of the German story, who visited the court of Venus, the Goddess of Love, and there forgot everything but pleasure; but later he repented. The story is set to music in Wagner's opera. George was not the first, nor the last, to be saved from slackness and inspired to deeds of courage by a book. Compare his request to be set free with that of Bee in a former part of the story. What do you think about Nur's opinion on science and poetry?

Chapter XVII.

What is the "bezel" of a ring? And how would you like to go boating on a petroleum lake? There is a wonderful description of King Loc's journey through the sea cavern. Does it recall any piece of literature, prose or verse, song or story. There is a good picture in the story of the meeting of George and his rival. Aristotle was a Greek philosopher who knew almost everything there was to be known. If King Loc had belonged to our time we should call him a "sport." But it was too much to hurl Bee's name at him without any preparation. On the whole the shadows of the story appear to be lifting in this chapter, don't they?

Chapter XVIII.

John's exclamation was not quite polite. If he did not see a ghost he might have guessed that it was an angel. The people had given a natural cause for the disappearance of George, but explained Bee's absence in a more wonderful and mysterious way, with a touch of poetry. The home-coming of George has various effects, according to the character of the people he meets. Freeheart back again, too, and still at his old game of "making a song about it"! The light grows brighter and brighter.

Chapter XIX.

It was the common people who were expected to know all about the habits of the dwarfs. Glauce is good fun and a clever girl would love to act her part in a play; she is by no means unimportant in the story. Cider added to oats for a horse! I wonder what Glauce meant by "drinking fair"? And what the neighbours said afterwards about her late husband's story?

Chapter XX.

An "espadon" must be a terrible weapon, judging by its name. Avalon lies at the farthest verge of the western sea and is the last home of all good knights, including King Arthur:

> *The island-valley of Avilion;*
> *Where falls not hail, or rain, or any snow,*
> *Nor ever wind blows loudly: but it lies*
> *Deep-meadowed, happy, fair with orchard-lawns*
> *And bowery hollows crowned with summer sea.*

And Thule is the northernmost land of all the world. Freeheart's ideas of costume are quite original; but his notion of wine-inspired courage is not so praiseworthy. He is, however, a better diplomatist than George, and has a very charming way of telling the young lover that he has been foolishly rude. George's entry, reception, and meeting with little King Loc make a splendid moving picture. Disappointment in love has not soured the little king, but has made him something of a poet; and how gently he reproves the hot-headed George! How kind George is, too, in the midst of his happiness. And all ends in mock-heroics and good fun.

Chapter XXI.

The last scene of all makes one long to have a play based upon this story. Who would not be proud to act King Loc and have such a lofty mind? It would be difficult, of course, to get together such a wedding present as he gave Bee, but the players could easily agree to play the game of "Let's pretend," as Shakespeare did when he hung up a card, on the curtain, bearing the words, "This is a wood."

A true story? Well—what is it all about? It is a story of mother-love, child-love, and lover's love. It is full of kindliness, courage, gaiety, forgiveness, compassion, helpfulness, resource, and fortitude. And these things have always been true, are true to-day and will be true long, long after we all reach the "island valley of Avilion." So, what greater truth could we ask for?

We give here for purposes of enjoyment and comparison a prose story and a poem, both of which tell the story of the Greek maiden who was carried off to the dark Underworld, but who, unlike Bee, became the bride of its king; also another story of dwarfs and their ways.

THE SORROW OF DEMETER

In the fields of Enna, in the happy island of Sicily, the beautiful Persephone was playing with the girls who lived there with her. She was the daughter of the Lady Demeter, and every one loved them both; for Demeter was good and kind to all, and no one could be more gentle and merry than Persephone. She and her companions were gathering flowers from the field, to make crowns for their long flowing hair. They had picked many roses and lilies and hyacinths which grew in clusters around them, when Persephone thought she saw a splendid flower far off; and away she ran, as fast as she could, to get it. It was a beautiful narcissus, with a hundred heads springing from one stem; and the perfume which came from its flowers gladdened the broad heaven above, and the earth and sea around it. Eagerly Persephone stretched out her hand to take this splendid prize, when the earth opened. and a chariot stood before her drawn by four coal-black horses; and in the chariot there was a man with a dark and solemn face, which looked as though he could never smile, and as though he had never been happy. In a moment he got out of his chariot, seized Persephone round the waist, and put her on the seat by his side. Then he touched the horses with his whip, and they drew the chariot down into the great gulf, and the earth closed over them again.

Presently the girls who had been playing with Persephone came up to the place where the beautiful narcissus was growing; but they could not see her anywhere. And they said, "Here is the very flower which she ran to pick, and there is no place here where she can be hiding." Still for a long time they searched for her through the fields of Enna; and when the evening was come, they went home to tell the Lady Demeter that they could not tell what had become of Persephone.

Very terrible was the sorrow of Demeter when she was told that her child was lost. She put a dark robe on her shoulders, and took a flaming torch in her hand, and went over land and sea to look for Persephone. But no one could tell her where she was gone. When ten days were passed she met Hekate, and asked her about her child; but Hekate said, "I heard her voice, as she cried out when some one seized her; but I did not see it with my eyes, and so I know not where she is gone." Then she went to Helios, and said to him, "O Helios, tell me about my child. Thou seest everything on the earth, sitting in the bright sun." Then Helios said to Demeter, "I pity thee for thy great sorrow, and I will tell thee the truth. It is Hades who has taken away Persephone to be his wife in the dark and gloomy land which lies beneath in the earth."

Then the rage of Demeter was more terrible than her sorrow had been; and she would not stay in the palace of Zeus, on the great Thessalian hill, because it was Zeus who had allowed Hades to take away Persephone. So she went down from Olympus, and wandered on a long way until she came to Eleusis, just as the sun was going down into his golden cup behind the dark blue hills. There Demeter sat down close to a fountain, where the water bubbled out from the green turf and fell into a clear basin, over which some dark olive-trees spread their branches.

Just then the daughters of Keleos, the king of Eleusis, came to the fountain with pitchers on their heads to draw water; and when they saw Demeter, they knew from her face that she must have some great grief; and they spoke kindly to her, and asked if they could do anything to help her. Then she told them how she had lost and was searching for her child; and they said, "Come home and live with us: and our father and mother will give you everything that you can want, and do all that they can to soothe your sorrow." So Demeter went down to the house of Keleos, and she stayed there for a whole year. And all this time, although the daughters of Keleos were very gentle and kind to her, she went on mourning and weeping for Persephone.

She never laughed or smiled, and scarcely ever did she speak to any one, because of her great grief. And even the earth, and the things which grow on the earth, mourned for the sorrow which had come upon Demeter. There was no fruit upon the trees, no corn came up in the fields, and no flowers blossomed in the gardens. And Zeus looked down from his high Thessalian hill, and saw that everything must die unless he could soothe the grief and anger of Demeter. So he sent Hermes down to Hades, the dark and stern king, to bid him send Persephone to see her mother Demeter. But before Hades let her go, he gave her a pomegranate to eat, because he did not wish her to stay away from him always, and he knew that she must come back if she tasted but one of the pomegranate seeds. Then the great chariot was brought before the door of the palace, and Hermes touched with his whip the coal-black horses, and away they went as swiftly as the wind, until they came close to Eleusis. Then Hermes left Persephone, and the coal-black horses drew the chariot away again to the dark home of King Hades.

The sun was sinking down in the sky when Hermes left Persephone, and as she came near to the fountain she saw some-one sitting near it in a long black robe, and she knew that it must be her mother who still wept and mourned for her child. And as Demeter heard the rustling of her dress, she lifted up her face, and Persephone stood before her.

Then the joy of Demeter was greater, as she clasped her daughter to her breast, than her grief and her sorrow had been. Again and again she held Persephone in her arms, and asked her about all that had happened to her. And she said, "Now that you are come back to me, I shall never let you go away again; Hades shall not have my child to live with him in his dreary kingdom." But Persephone said, "It may not be so, my mother; I cannot stay with you always; for before Hermes brought me away to see you, Hades gave me a pomegranate, and I have eaten some of the seeds; and after tasting the seed I must go back to him again when six months have passed by. And indeed, I am not afraid to go; for although Hades never smiles or laughs, and everything in his palace is dark and gloomy, still he is very kind to me: and I think that he feels almost happy since I have been his wife. But do not be sorry, my mother, for he has promised to let me come up and stay with you for six months in every year, and the other six months I must spend with him in the land which lies beneath the earth."

So Demeter was comforted for her daughter Persephone, and the earth and all the things that grew in it felt that her anger and sorrow had passed away. Once more the trees bore their fruits, the flowers spread out their sweet blossoms in the garden, and the golden corn waved like the sea under the soft summer breeze. So the six months passed happily away, and then Hermes came with the coal-black horses to take Persephone to the dark land. And she said to her mother, "Do not weep much; the gloomy king whose wife I am is so kind to me that I cannot be really unhappy; and in six months more he will let me come to you again." But still, whenever the time came round for Persephone to go back to Hades, Demeter thought of the happy days when her child was a merry girl playing with her companions and gathering the bright flowers in the beautiful plains of Enna.

THE KING OF THE GOLDEN MOUNTAIN
FROM "GRIMM'S FAIRY TALES"

There was once a merchant who had only one child, a son, that was very young, and barely able to run alone. He had two richly laden ships then making a voyage upon the seas, in which he had embarked all his wealth, in the hope of making great gains, when the news came that both were lost. Thus from being a rich man he became all at once so very poor that nothing was left to him but one small plot of land; and there he often went in an evening to take his walk, and ease his mind of a little of his trouble.

One day, as he was roaming along in a brown study, thinking with no great comfort on what he had been and what he now was, and was like to be, all on a sudden there stood before him a little rough-looking black dwarf. "Prithee, friend, why so sorrowful?" said he to the merchant; "what is it you take so deeply to heart?" "If you could do me any good I would willingly tell you," said the merchant. "Who knows but I may?" said the little man: "tell me what ails you, and perhaps you will find I may be of some use." Then the merchant told him how all his wealth was gone to the bottom of the sea, and how he had nothing left but that little plot of land. "Oh! trouble not yourself about that," said the dwarf; "only undertake to bring me here, twelve years hence, whatever meets you first on your going home, and I will give you as much as you please." The merchant thought this was no great thing to ask; that it would most likely be his dog or his cat, or something of that sort, but forgot his little boy Heinel; so he agreed to the bargain, and signed and sealed the bond to do what was asked of him.

But as he drew near home, his little boy was so glad to see him that he crept behind him, and laid fast hold of his legs, and looked up in his face and laughed. Then the father started, trembling with fear and horror, and saw what it was that he had bound himself to do; but as no gold was come, he made himself easy, by thinking that it was only a joke that the dwarf was playing him, and that, at any rate, when the money came, he should see the bearer, and would not take it in.

About a month afterwards he went upstairs into a lumberroom to look for some old iron, that he might sell it and raise a little money; and there, instead of his iron, he saw a large pile of gold lying on the floor. At the sight of this he was overjoyed, and forgetting all about his son, went into trade again, and became a richer merchant than before.

Meantime little Heinel grew up, and as the end of the twelve years drew near the merchant began to call to mind his bond, and became very sad and thoughtful; so that care and sorrow were written upon his face. The boy one day asked what was the matter, but his father would not tell for some time; at last, however, he said that he had, without knowing it, sold him for gold to a little, ugly-looking, black dwarf, and that the twelve years were coming round when he must keep his word. Then Heinel said, "Father, give yourself very little trouble about that; I shall be too much for the little man."

When the time came, the father and son went out together to the place agreed upon: and the son drew a circle on the ground, and set himself and his father in the middle of it. The little black dwarf soon came, and walked round and round about the circle, but could not find any way to get into it, and he either could not, or dared not, jump over it. At last the boy said to him, "Have you anything to say to us, my friend, or what do you want?" Now Heinel had found a friend in a good fairy, that was fond of him, and had told him what to do; for this fairy knew what good luck was in store for him. "Have you brought me what you said you would?" said the dwarf to the merchant. The old man held his tongue, but Heinel said again, "What do you want here?" The dwarf said, "I come to talk with your father, not with you." "You have cheated and taken in my father," said the son; "pray give him up his bond at once." "Fair and softly," said the little old man; "right is right. I have paid my money, and your father has had it, and spent it; so be so good as to let me have what I paid it for." "You must have my consent to that first," said Heinel; "so please to step in here, and let us talk it over." The old man grinned, and showed his teeth, as if he should have been very glad to get into the circle if he could. Then at last, after a long talk, they came to terms. Heinel agreed that his father must give him up, and that so far the dwarf should have his way: but, on the other hand, the fairy had told Heinel what fortune was in store for him, if he followed his own course; and he did not choose to be given up to his hump-backed friend, who seemed so anxious for his company.

So, to make a sort of drawn battle of the matter, it was settled that Heinel should be put into an open boat, that lay on the sea-shore hard by; that the father should push him off with his own hand, and that he should thus be set adrift, and left to the bad or good luck of wind and weather. Then he took leave of his father, and set himself in the boat; but before it got far off a wave struck it, and it fell with one side low in the water, so the merchant thought that poor Heinel was lost, and went home very sorrowful, while the dwarf went his way, thinking that at any rate he had had his revenge.

The boat, however, did not sink, for the good fairy took care of her friend, and soon raised the boat up again, and it went safely on. The young man sat safe within, till at length it ran ashore upon an unknown land. As he jumped upon the shore he saw before him a beautiful castle, but empty and dreary within, for it was enchanted. "Here," said he to himself, "must I find the prize the good fairy told me of." So he once more searched the whole palace through, till at last he found a white snake, lying coiled up on a cushion in one of the chambers.

Now the white snake was an enchanted princess; and she was very glad to see him, and said, "Are you at last come to set me free? Twelve long years have I waited here for the fairy to bring you hither as she promised, for you alone can save me. This night twelve men will come: their faces will be black, and they will be dressed in chain armour. They will ask what you do here, but give no answer; and let them do what they will, beat, whip, pinch, prick, or torment you, bear all; only speak not a word, and at twelve o'clock they must go away. The second night twelve others will come: and the third night twenty-four, who will even cut off your head; but at the twelfth hour of that night their power is gone, and I shall be free, and will come and bring you the water of life, and will wash you with it, and bring you back to life and health." And all came to pass as she had said; Heinel bore all, and spoke not a word; and the third night the princess came, and fell on his neck and kissed him. Joy and gladness burst forth throughout the castle, the wedding was celebrated, and he was crowned king of the Golden Mountain.

They lived together very happily, and the queen had a son. And thus eight years had passed over their heads, when the king thought of his father; and he began to long to see him once again. But the queen was against his going, and said, "I know well that misfortunes will come upon us if you go." However, he gave her no rest till she agreed. At his going away she gave him a wishing-ring, and said, "Take this ring, and put it on your finger, whatever you wish it will bring you: only promise never to make use of it to bring me hence to your father's house." Then he said he would do what she asked, and put the ring on his finger, and wished himself near the town where his father lived.

Heinel found himself at the gates in a moment; but the guards would not let him go in, because he was so strangely clad. So he went up to a neighbouring hill, where a shepherd dwelt, and borrowed his old frock, and thus passed unknown into the town. When he came to his father's house, he said he was his son; but the merchant would not believe him, and said he had had but one son, his poor Heinel, who he knew was long since dead: and as he was only dressed like a poor shepherd, he would not even give him anything to eat. The king, however, still vowed that he was his son, and said, "Is there no mark by which you would know me if I am really your son?" "Yes," said his mother, "our Heinel had a mark like a raspberry on his right arm." Then he showed them the mark, and they knew that what he had said was true.

He next told them how he was king of the Golden Mountain, and was married to a princess, and had a son seven years old. But the merchant said, "That can never be true; he must be a fine king truly who travels about in a shepherd's frock!" At this the son was vexed; and forgetting his word, turned his ring, and wished for his queen and son. In an instant they stood before him; but the queen wept, and said he had broken his word, and bad luck would follow. He did all he could to soothe her, and she at last seemed to be appeased; but she was not so in truth, and was only thinking how she should punish him.

One day he took her to walk with him out of the town, and showed her the spot where the boat was set adrift upon the wide waters. Then he sat himself down, and said, "I am very much tired; sit by me, I will rest my head in your lap, and sleep awhile." As soon as he had fallen asleep, however, she drew the ring from his finger, and crept softly away, and wished herself and her son at home in their kingdom. And when he awoke he found himself alone, and saw that the ring was gone from his finger. "I can never go back to my father's house," said he, "they would say I am a sorcerer: I will journey forth into the world, till I come again to my kingdom."

So saying, he set out and travelled till he came to a hill, where three giants were sharing their father's goods; and as they saw him pass, they cried out and said, "Little men have sharp wits; he shall part the goods between us." Now there was a sword, that cut off an enemy's head whenever the wearer gave the words, "Heads off!" a cloak, that made the owner invisible, or gave him any form he pleased; and a pair of boots that carried the wearer wherever he wished. Heinel said they must first let him try these wonderful things, then he might know how to set a value upon them. Then they gave him the cloak, and he wished himself a fly, and in a moment he was a fly. "The cloak is very well," said he; "now give me the sword." "No," said they; "not unless you undertake not to say, 'Heads off!' for if you do, we are all dead men." So they gave it him, charging him to try it on a tree. He next asked for the boots also; and the moment he had all three in his power, he wished himself at the Golden Mountain; and there he was at once. So the giants were left behind with no goods to share or quarrel about.

As Heinel came near his castle he heard the sound of merry music; and the people around told him that his queen was about to marry another husband. Then he threw his cloak around him, and passed through the castle-hall, and placed himself by the side of his queen, where no one saw him. But when anything to eat was put upon her plate, he took it away and ate it himself; and when a glass of wine was handed to her, he took it and drank it: and thus, though they kept on giving her meat and drink, her plate and cup were always empty.

Upon this fear and remorse came over her, and she went into her chamber alone, and sat there weeping; and he followed her there. "Alas!" said she to herself, "was I not once set free? why then does this enchantment still seem to bind me?"

"False and fickle one!" said he, "one indeed came who set thee free, and he is now near thee again; but how have you used him? ought he to have had such treatment from thee?" Then he went out and sent away the company, and said the wedding was at an end, for that he was come back to the kingdom. But the princes, peers, and great men mocked at him. However, he would enter into no parley with them, but only asked them if they would go in peace or not. Then they turned upon him and tried to seize him; but he drew his sword; "Heads off!" cried he; and with the word, the traitors' heads fell before him, and Heinel was once more king of the Golden Mountain.

PERSEPHONE[1]

I

She stepped upon Sicilian grass,
Demeter's daughter, fresh and fair;
A child of light, a radiant lass,
And gamesome as the morning air.
The daffodils were fair to see,
They nodded lightly on the lea,
Persephone—Persephone!
Lo! one she marked of fairer growth
Than orchis or anemone:
For it the maiden left them both,
And parted from her company.
Drawn nigh she deemed it fairer still,
And stooped to gather by the rill
The daffodil, the daffodil.
What ailed the meadow that it shook?
What ailed the air of Sicily?
She wandered by the prattling brook,
And trembled with the trembling lea.
"The coal-black horses rise—they rise:
O Mother, Mother!" low she cries—
Persephone—Persephone!
"O light, light, light!" she cried, "farewell;
The coal-black horses wait for me.
O shade of shades, where must I dwell,

---

1   In some forms of this story the maiden is called Proser-
pina and her mother Ceres. Tennyson tells the story in his poem
"Demeter."

Demeter, Mother, far from thee!
Ah, fated doom that I fulfil!
Ah, fateful flower beside the rill!
The daffodil, the daffodil!"
What ails her that she comes not home?
Demeter seeks her far and wide,
And gloomy-browed doth ceaseless roam
From many a morn till eventide.
"My life, immortal though it be,
Is nought," she cried, "for want of thee,
Persephone—Persephone!"
"Meadows of Enna, let the rain
No longer drop to feed your rills,
Nor dew refresh the fields again,
With all their nodding daffodils!
Fade, fade and droop, O lilied lea,
Where thou, dear heart, wast reft from me—
Persephone—Persephone!"

II

She reigns upon her dusky throne,
'Mid shades of heroes dread to see;
Among the dead she breathes alone,
Persephone—Persephone!
Or seated on the Elysian hill
She dreams of earthly daylight still,
And murmurs of the daffodil.
A voice in Hades soundeth clear,
The shadows mourn and flit below;
It cries—"Thou Lord of Hades, hear,
And let Demeter's daughter go.
The tender corn upon the lea
Droops in her golden gloom when she
Cries for her lost Persephone.
"From land to land she raging flies,
The green fruit falleth in her wake,

And harvest fields beneath her eyes
To earth the grain unripened shake.
Arise and set the maiden free;
Why should the world such sorrow dree[2]
By reason of Persephone?"
He takes the cleft pomegranate seeds,
"Love, eat with me this parting day;"
Then bids them fetch the coal-black steeds—
"Demeter's daughter, wouldst away?"
The gates of Hades set her free;
"She will return full soon," saith he—
"My wife, my wife Persephone."
Low laughs the dark king on his throne—
"I gave her of pomegranate seeds;"
Demeter's daughter stands alone
Upon the fair Eleusian meads.
Her mother meets her. "Hail!" saith she;
"And doth our daylight dazzle thee,
My love, my child Persephone?
"What moved thee, daughter, to forsake
Thy fellow-maids that fatal morn,
And give thy dark lord power to take
Thee living to his realm forlorn?"
Her lips reply without her will,
As one address who slumbereth still—
"The daffodil, the daffodil!"
Her eyelids droop with light oppressed,
And sunny wafts that round her stir,
Her cheek is on her mother's breast,
Demeter's kisses comfort her.
Calm Queen of Hades, art thou she
Who stepped so lightly on the lea—
Persephone, Persephone?
When, in her destined course, the moon

---

2   Dree: endure or bear.

Meets the deep shadow of this world,
And labouring on doth seem to swoon
Through awful wastes of dimness whirled—
Emerged at length, no trace hath she
Of that dark hour of destiny,
Still silvery sweet—Persephone.
The greater world may near the less,
And draw it through her weltering shade,
But not one biding trace impress
Of all the darkness that she made;
The greater soul that draweth thee
Hath left his shadow plain to see
On thy fair face, Persephone!
Demeter sighs, but sure 'tis well
The wife should love her destiny;
They part, and yet, as legends tell,
She mourns her lost Persephone;
While chant the maids of Enna still—
"O fateful flower, beside the rill—
The daffodil, the daffodil!"

JEAN INGELOW (1820-89).

THE WRITER OF THE STORY OF BEE

The best way to learn something about the author of *Bee* is to study with care the portrait given as the frontispiece of this book. You shall form your own opinion of the man from the artist's drawing and that opinion will depend greatly upon the amount of enjoyment and the number of ideas you have got from his story.

His name is sufficient guide to his nationality, and you will know by easy guesswork that you have been reading a translation of his tale; but the change from French to English is so well made that not much is lost of the charm of the story as Anatole France wrote it. The best way to judge his work is, of course, to read it in French.

Anatole France is not, like Hans Andersen, a recognised fairy-tale writer, which from our point of view seems a pity, because he has the light touch which does not crush the gossamer or brush the dust from the wings of the butterfly. It is of no use having a heavy touch if you are dealing with things like Queen Mab's Wagon.

> *Her wagon-spokes made of long spinners' legs.*
> *The cover of the wings of grasshoppers,*
> *Her traces of the smallest spider's web,*
> *Her whip of crickets' bone, the lash of film;*
> *Her wagoner a small grey-coated gnat,*
> *Her chariot is an empty hazel-nut*
> *Made by the joiner squirrel, or old grub,*
> *Time out o' mind the fairies' coach-makers.*

One of our own writers, John Ruskin, wrote one fairy tale called The King of the Golden River, and the rest of his writings, like those of Anatole France, were for grown-up readers. There are some people who think that Ruskin's fairy tale is one of the best of its kind ever written, and Bee: the Princess of the Dwarfs is quite worthy to stand beside it. You may care to compare the two in matters of detail and style, and will find the work very interesting indeed; and you will remember that it is quite fair to compare these two stories, for they were both invented or "made-up" by their authors all out of their own heads.

Most of the old fairy tales, like Cinderella, seem to have grown like the cabbages, or, shall we say, the roses. They have been told again and again by one person after another as the years rolled by and they were well known before anyone set them down in print. In a sense, Bee and The King of the Golden River are not true fairy tales, but you will agree that they are very good imitations of the old models.

Anatole France, whose real surname is Thibault, was the son of a bookseller in Paris, and was born so long ago as 1844. He was brought up among books and among clever men who came to his father's shop not only to buy books but to discuss them. It is not surprising that when he grew up he should begin to write books.

As for his thoughts about things in general, you will find them all in the pages of *Bee: the Princess of the Dwarfs*.

www.ingramcontent.com/pod-product-compliance
Lightning Source LLC
Chambersburg PA
CBHW030536180626
46810CB00005B/1893